MORE BOOKS FROM THE SAGER GROUP

The Swamp: Deceit and Corruption in the CIA
An Elizabeth Petrov Thriller (Book 1)
by Jeff Grant

Chains of Nobility: Brotherhood of the Mamluks (Book 1-3)
by Brad Graft

Meeting Mozart: A Novel Drawn from the Secret Diaries of Lorenzo Da Ponte
by Howard Jay Smith

Death Came Swiftly: Novel About the Tay Bridge Disaster of 1879
by Bill Abrams

A Boy and His Dog in Hell: And Other Stories
by Mike Sager

Miss Havilland: A Novel
by Gay Daly

The Orphan's Daughter: A Novel
by Jan Cherubin

Lifeboat No. 8: Surviving the Titanic
by Elizabeth Kaye

Hunting Marlon Brando: A True Story
by Mike Sager

See our entire library at <u>TheSagerGroup.net</u>

PARTY SCHOOL

A NOVEL

JON HART

Party School, a Novel

Copyright © 2022 Jon Hart

All rights reserved.

Published in the United States of America.

Cover and Interior Designed by Siori Kitajima, PatternBased.com

Cataloging-in-Publication data for this book is available from the Library of Congress

ISBN-13:
eBook: 978-1-950154-87-6
Paperback: 978-1-950154-88-3

Published by The Sager Group LLC
(TheSagerGroup.net)

PARTY SCHOOL

A NOVEL

JON HART

THE SAGER GROUP

Artifex Te Adiuva

CONTENTS

AUGUST

No biggie. I was at another party I didn't want to be at. Everyone had returned from their ridiculous summer homes, and my high school class was back for one last big one before we all went away to school. FYI: I wasn't coming back from anywhere—no second home for me. I was working, bussing tables all summer, every day. It was fun, well, sometimes, and I was making coin.

We were at the usual spot, Castleton's Castle, an insane stone fortress, which was built before the Revolutionary War. It's a national landmark. No one's allowed inside, but there are a few picnic tables in the back. It's perched on a hill, overlooking the river, in walking distance for everyone in Castleton. As long as we didn't do anything stupid like puke our brains out, the village's private security force let us be.

I don't want to be here. I shouldn't be here. I'm done. I just finished a double, and I have another tomorrow. And I've already heard what these characters have to say a zillion times before—and you probably have too. High school kids. What do they know? High school kids with money. Yeah, they have it figured out because they never had to figure it out.

No, I haven't figured it out.

Anyway, I couldn't bear to hear these kids talk about their big plans. But Rosemary wanted to stop by, so here we are. Yeah, Rosemary. She's my girlfriend. She calls the shots.

As Rosemary did her thing, I stepped away and sat on one of the benches overlooking the river. I enjoyed the breeze and started doing what I do: strumming words together.

> *No stars in the sky as we fake goodbyes.*
> *We all make promises that turn out to be lies.*

As this—whatever it was—ran through my mind, I was interrupted. TTK, one of Castleton's *it* kids, took a seat next to me, a plastic cup of beer in each hand.

"You want one?" he asked. TTK is short for The Taliban Kid. He has an insane story. His parents had been in the Taliban, and he's an orphan. One of our classmates, Davis Palmer, discovered TTK on Instagram and recruited him to Castleton. Davis wrote his college essay about the experience, and it helped him get accepted to an *it* school. An *it* school is a school that everyone wants to attend. I won't bore you with the names. You already know them, and I'm sick of hearing them. Anyway, there are different categories of *it* schools. There are elite *it* schools, medium *it* schools, barely *it* schools, and wannabe *it* schools.

"I'm good," I told TTK. I wasn't. After a day of bussing tables, I wanted no part of this mess. I just wanted to swim into Rosemary's delightful green eyes. Alcohol would just make me sleepy. I wasn't much of a drinker anyway. Even during the school year, I worked at the restaurant a lot. It felt like I was there more than at school. If I were hungover, I just couldn't deal.

"What's your name again?" TTK asked with a friendly smile. We'd run against one another for class secretary freshman year, which now seemed like a lifetime ago. There were seven other candidates. Why on earth would so many people want to be class secretary? We wanted extracurriculars for our college applications.

Yeah, we're all frauds.

In case you're wondering: I finished sixth, at least officially. Two other candidates on the ballot announced at the last minute that they were no longer interested. I was never interested, but I stuck it out. TTK won decisively. This kid was going places.

"Dylan," I answered, pretending not to be annoyed.

"Dylan Mills. Of course, I know your name; I was just being stupid." Ironic. TTK was anything but that.

I forced a smile, but it was probably a grimace.

I didn't know TTK's actual name. No one did. Most probably didn't even know what TTK was an abbreviation for. TTK did have a certain ring to it. TTK had done an incredible job of assimilating into Castleton, way better than I had.

"How's your night going?" I asked. I thought I should speak to at least one person while I was there.

"Not that great," TTK said dejectedly.

"What's up?"

"Melissa and I broke up."

"What happened?" I knew Melissa vaguely, which meant we passed each other in the school hallway.

"We're going away to different schools. We figured it'd be easier to start over with a clean slate."

"Yeah, I can see that," I nodded, pretending again. I didn't see it. If TTK could survive whatever hell he'd been through, he could survive a temporary separation. C'mon! Thanksgiving was three months away.

"What's the plan for you and Rosemary?"

The question was a firm punch to the gut. It was what I'd been desperately trying to avoid. We had no plan. Rosemary was my plan. Since I had no answer, and I didn't want to answer, I didn't.

I exchanged meaningless pleasantries for maybe ten minutes, but it felt a hundred times longer.

"I'll hit you up on the 'gram," someone promised.

I wasn't on the 'gram.

"Yeah, I'd like to do a road trip for the big game," I promised.

I didn't have a driver's license, much less a car, so this was very unlikely.

"I've got your text. Keep an eye out."

I'm not holding my breath.

"Can't wait to see you at Thanksgiving."

What else could I say? I'd planned on working at Luncheonette, the restaurant I worked at, on Thanksgiving. It would be packed, and tips would be nice.

"What's the name of your school again?"

I pretended not to hear that one.

Fact: If it weren't for the reality that I worked at Luncheonette, Castleton's most popular dining spot, I probably wouldn't see these people again, and I didn't care. Before we go any further, understand this: Castleton is not a town. It's a village. For whatever reason, the Castleton big shots—and just about everyone thinks they're one in this place—want it that way. Anyway, Castleton is swanky, postcard perfect; a One-Percenter suburban haven dotted with matching white colonials and perfectly manicured lawns. In the center, matching black streetlights line its immaculate, mostly empty sidewalks. Our village's credo should be "People make things messy." Castleton High is public, but it's nicer than the priciest private schools. Castleton High has an equestrian team and *two* polo teams: water polo and the one played on horseback.

"Do you want to get out of here?" Rosemary asked.

Suddenly, I had a tremendous surge of energy.

"Absolutely not," I deadpanned. "Let's stay 'til the bitter end."

"Let's go. You're too funny."

I wasn't. I was tired, I was tired of waiting for her, but I pretended that I was up for anything and that I wasn't needy. No one likes needy. I don't like needy, but I was needy.

We walked down Castle Hill where Rosemary had parked her car. I suggested an Uber, but Rosemary swore that she'd limited herself to a few sips of beer a few hours ago. Rosemary wasn't much of a drinker, so I believed her. When the opportunity arose—and it wasn't that often—Rosemary smoked weed. She said it mellowed her. After I got nauseous from some cannabis gummy bears, I stayed clear of grass. I probably shouldn't have, but I allowed Rosemary to drive. Rosemary had a way. And, yeah, as I said, she calls the shots. I didn't drive. I still needed to get my driver's license. I keep telling myself that, but I just haven't done it. Anyway, Rosemary's house was less than a mile away. We could drive there with our eyes shut. But once we got to her house, Rosemary cruised right past it.

"Where are we going there, Rosebud?" I asked in my corny, cutesy voice.

"It's a surprise." Rosemary loved surprises.

Rosemary's family cottage in Calm Lake was just forty-five minutes away, but the ride went fast because we sang Barry Manilow the entire way. Something to know about my family: We love Barry. I was practically raised on the man, and I'd turned Rosemary on to him. On my parents' third date, my father took my mother to a Barry concert. Barry picked my parents out of the audience, and Barry and my father wound up serenading her. At the time, my mother was far from sold on my father. After Barry, she was. Here's something I ponder often: If it weren't for Barry Manilow, I might not be here. Anyway, if you're not familiar, Barry's awesome, but his songs often sound similar and cover the same territory: couples defying the odds to find eternal love, almost always in a steady downpour. Be forewarned: Barry is freakin' addictive. Once you start listening, you can't stop.

Calm Lake felt like another hemisphere. I tried to get there as much as possible, which wound up being almost never because I was always working, and I preferred to be there when Rosemary's parents were not. It's not that her parents didn't like me. They just didn't like me. They were polite, but in the way that you're supposed to be to the waitstaff. Yeah, of course, I tried to win them over. I brought them amazing white chocolate chip cookies from Luncheonette, and I mowed their lawn, and I hate to mow lawns. But whatever I did, it didn't matter. As much as I hate to admit it, I often felt like a placeholder until something better came along.

Calm Lake was pitch black. If I didn't know that Calm Lake had insane security, at least during the summer, I'd be terrified. Rosemary grabbed a blanket from inside. We went out to our spot on her porch patio, which overlooked the enormous lake. We snuggled, listened to the water and whatever else was out there, and looked up at the crescent moon and beyond.

Yeah, outer space.

When I was a kid, I thought I'd be there. After a fourth-grade science teacher told my parents that I had some potential in astronomy, my parents sent me off to space camp at Cape Canaveral for two weeks. When I returned, a spaceship was in our backyard, kind of. My parents had hired a local carpenter to build a spaceship. In the following weeks, we'd dressed up in silver space suits, sat in our fake spaceship, and counted down as if we were about to blast off. Yeah, I know it's all very goofy, but my parents were serious. Our destination wasn't the moon. My parents were grooming me for Mars.

We never got off the ground.

Eventually, we learned that my allergies would make any space mission impossible. Heck, when we took a helicopter ride, my entire family vomited.

"Did your parents really want you to go to Mars?" Rosemary asked for what seemed like the zillionth time.

"I know you know the answer to that question."

"I know. I know. But how could you get to Mars? You don't even have a driver's license."

We both laughed.

"If you were there, I'd go to Mars." Hokey. It's my thing. Sue me.

"Well, that's good," Rosemary laughed. "I wouldn't want to be on Mars alone."

Rosemary rested her head on my shoulder, and we sat, enjoying an incredible silence. I wanted this moment to never end.

"I've been thinking," Rosemary began slowly.

Suddenly, our moment was gone, and I desperately wanted it back.

"I haven't."

Rosemary ignored my lame quip. Suddenly, I wasn't so funny.

"Melissa and TTK broke up. So did Sean and Dara. And Tom and Steve."

I didn't like where this was going. I hated where this was going.

"And . . ." Rosemary stopped abruptly. I didn't want another *and*. "Everything's changing."

"Well . . . we don't have to change."

Right after I said it, I reminded myself to stop being needy. Pronto.

"But we are. We're leaving Castleton. We're going to different schools."

"Yes," I somehow managed to reply calmly. "It will not be easy."

"My mother says that we shouldn't limit ourselves."

"My mother thinks you're amazing."

"I think your mother's amazing."

We were having a mother contest. Fun, fun times.

"What else is your mother saying?"

Right after I asked, I regretted asking. Who cares what her mother was saying? Well, unfortunately, I care.

"Well, she thinks we should meet new people."

"I love meeting people. I'm all for that!"

"No you don't."

Rosemary punched my shoulder playfully, and we both laughed. But then Rosemary turned serious again. "She thinks we should see other people."

Suddenly, I was nauseous. I would have screamed "No!" at the top of my lungs, but all the air was sucked out of me. Somehow, I gathered myself and resorted to reason.

"You think we should break up because your mother wants us to?" I asked calmly.

"It's not breaking up. It's seeing other people!"

I could breathe again, kind of.

"It sounds like breaking up."

"Well, I don't want to break up."

"Me neither."

It was a false alarm. Yeah, I could breathe.

"But . . ." Rosemary began. I braced myself. My father always told me that rarely anything good comes after *but*. "They have a point."

"They?" I asked.

"My father agrees with my mother."

"Great! He's against me too?"

"He's not against you. He's always sticking up for you."

"If he's sticking up for me, someone's sticking me down."

"No one's sticking you down! I just think we should be open to new experiences."

What did this all mean?

I didn't care what Rosemary's parents wanted. I mean I did care—just as long as they wanted us to be us. And I didn't care about new experiences. I didn't say any of this though.

Instead, I looked directly into Rosemary's wonderful green eyes.

"I love you, Rosemary Silversmith."

"I love you too, but . . ." Oh no, another *but*.

"What?"

"We must grow."

*

Just after sunrise, Rosemary drove us back to Castleton, and she dropped me off at Luncheonette in plenty of time for my shift. Rosemary was leaving tomorrow for her *it* school, the same one her parents went to, and she had last-minute errands. I was working at Luncheonette right until I had to depart for North South—yeah, my school's unfortunate name. In case you're wondering, North South isn't an *it* school, not even close, but we'll get to that. I hadn't done much preparation for going away. Part of me, well, most of me, wanted to bail, work at Luncheonette, and figure things out.

More specifically, I wanted to figure out how I could stay closer to Rosemary.

I powered through my shift with the aid of Luncheonette's potent, delicious coffee, but it wasn't a good shift. I was at Luncheonette—but I wasn't. I couldn't stop replaying my conversation with Rosemary from the previous night.

Rosemary wanted to meet new people.

Rosemary wanted to see other people.

Which was it?

Or was it both?

I tried to focus on the positive: Rosemary did not want to break up. Did I hear that correctly? Yes! Rosemary didn't want to break up. I repeated it in my head like a yoga chant.

I needed to go to a happy place, and I got there when I was summoned to assist with dishwashing duties, which reminded me of the first time we met—officially. Late one Sunday brunch, Rosemary poked her head into my dishwashing station, catching me by surprise. Why in the world was Rosemary Silversmith in Luncheonette's armpit?

"You got a minute?" she asked.

"Yeah, of course," I stammered. I didn't because we were slammed, but I'd make time.

I was taken aback. We'd seen each other at the Castleton pool, but we'd never actually spoken. I never knew she smelled this good. She made the armpit smell good.

Rosemary stepped just inside the door of my square crevice.

"Is everything all right . . . like with the food?" I asked awkwardly.

Dumb. Why would she go to the dishwasher to comment on the food?

"Everything's great. It always is. But, of course, you know that. You work here," Rosemary replied before pausing. "Well, we both go to Castleton High, and I see you here all the time, but we've never actually met. I just wanted to say hello. I'm Rosemary."

"I know. I'm Dylan."

I put forth my hand but then quickly retrieved it because it was covered with soap, water, and some gnarly things.

"I know."

"I guess we really know now." Rosemary smiled. "You're on the swim team, right?" she asked.

"No," I laughed nervously. "I'm in glee club."

"Well, kind of close."

"How so?"

"You need strong lungs for both."

"I guess you're right. I never thought about that."

"You work here every weekend, right?"

"Yeah. And sometimes a day or two during the week."

"That's so cool. I'd like to get a job, but I'm the hockey team's manager, and that takes up a ton of time."

I knew all this. I also knew that before she tore her ACL twice, Rosemary was the best hockey player in our class—male or female. She could really lay down a body check. In middle school, she once knocked out two guys in a single game. After her second ACL injury, the doctors recommended that she give up hockey.

Abruptly, Mr. Nillson, Luncheonette's manager, poked his head inside the station.

"Is there a problem?" he asked pointedly, not directing the question to either one of us.

"No," I muttered. "I . . ."

"I lost my earring," Rosemary interjected, smiling, pointing to the earring on her right ear. "Dylan found it somehow. I don't know how. I was just thanking him."

"Good work, Dylan," said Mr. Nillson.

From there, Rosemary and I progressed to bashful nods in the hallway to distracting library study sessions to bike rides home after school, even though Rosemary's house was out of my way. Sometimes, Rosemary would want to race.

"Catch me," she'd challenge as she sped away. I never did. Rosemary Silversmith was fast.

And I was firmly in the friend zone, but that was not all bad. At least I was in a zone.

When I got home from work in the early evening, my mother and father were waiting. FYI, my parents are divorced. It's still fresh, so I don't talk about it much. But no, it wasn't always hunky-dory in the Mills household, and I don't think I helped matters. If I were going to an *it* school, things might've been different. I would've made the family proud, provided some value to the Mills name. After the divorce, my father moved out and into an apartment outside of Castleton, where the rents are not so ridiculous.

But the divorce did the strangest thing.

My parents were together now more than ever, and they seemed happier—a lot happier. It was as if the pressure of "forever" was off, and they could just chill.

"How was the party?" my mother asked.

"It was a get-together," I answered.

Yeah, I was being a brat. I was exhausted, and I was still trying to figure out how to interpret Rosemary's plan. Was there even a plan? And I was preparing myself for what was coming. I was already counting the seconds.

"Have you and Rosemary discussed what you're going to do when you're both away at school?" my mother asked.

If you're timing, three short seconds.

I didn't want to answer, so I played dumb. "What do you mean?"

"Are you going to do the long-distance relationship thing?"

"I don't know."

"You don't know?" my father repeated accusingly. "Dana, he knows. He just doesn't want to share." My father said it as if I were intentionally inflicting pain.

I didn't, but they wanted an answer, so I gave them an answer.

"For the first three weeks of school, we're going to have no contact as we adjust to the college experience. We don't want to be living in our phones and not living."

It was a lie, a blatant lie, but I must admit that I liked the way the phrase sounded.

We don't want to be living in our phones and not living.

I couldn't bear to tell the truth, whatever the truth was, so I made something up. And I was buying myself three weeks.

By then, hopefully, Rosemary would come to her senses and stop growing, or whatever she was doing. It was only a matter of time. It might be a matter of hours. Minutes. Seconds. At any moment, her text would drop.

"Suddenly, you're so mature," my mother gushed in her game-show-contestant voice that made me nervous.

"Three weeks is a long time," my father said somberly.

It was too long.

"It's twenty-one days," I replied matter-of-factly with my best poker face.

"And what happens after that?" asked my father.

My parents wanted more. Always.

"We'll make it work."

"I know you will," said my mother. "Wonderful!"

I was miserable, and I excused myself so I could be alone with my lie. After maybe an hour, I returned downstairs and was mildly surprised to find Rosemary in our living room, which wasn't unusual at all. Our home had become Rosemary's, and we liked it that way. Her upbeat demeanor had a soothing effect on the normally anxious, now fractured Mills household. At this moment, though, I was not excited to have Rosemary Silversmith on our couch. I feared that my parents had revealed my lie, or Rosemary had updated them on our relationship status, whatever that was—or both.

"I didn't know you were here," I said nervously.

"I just came by to say goodbye to your parents," Rosemary replied.

"How long have you been here?" I felt like my parents conducting one of their interrogations.

"I don't know. Twenty minutes." Twenty minutes! It was practically an eternity, more than enough time for my parents to get intel. "Why?"

"Nothing, just wondering."

"Would you like to stay for dinner?" my mother asked.

Good news. My mother's mood was upbeat. Rosemary hadn't updated them on our status. Rosemary was a smart one. She knew that my parents wouldn't take it well.

"I'd love to, but I can't. My aunt and uncle and cousins are in to see me off. My parents have a special dinner planned."

No, I wasn't invited.

"You're practically adults!" my mother gushed.

"When Dylan starts doing his laundry more than once a month, he'll officially be an adult," cracked my father.

"Well, I better be off." Rosemary embraced each of my parents. "I just want to thank you for everything and tell you how much you've meant to me."

Why was Rosemary speaking in the past tense?

"You mean so much to us," my mother whimpered. Something to know about the Mills family: Tears come easily, anywhere, anytime, anyplace. If Barry's playing, odds are there are *mucho* tears. "You're like a daughter."

I would've shed tears too, but I was way too anxious.

What exactly did my parents tell Rosemary?

After the tears had subsided, I walked Rosemary to her car, cautiously.

"Let's take a quick ride," Rosemary directed. Perhaps Rosemary was changing her mind. We'd do the long-distance thing and get the forever that my parents didn't. Barry would write a song about us! We drove to the entrance of the Castle's service road and parked, and Rosemary looked directly into my eyes. No, it wasn't the look I wanted.

"Why'd you tell your parents that we weren't having contact for the first three weeks of school?" Rosemary asked with a sly grin.

"You know my mom. She was pestering me, and I was exhausted. It just came out."

I didn't want the truth. I couldn't bear to tell my parents that Rosemary and I were growing and seeing other people but not breaking up—whatever that all meant. "It was dumb."

"You know . . . it's actually a pretty smart idea."

"It's the worst idea. I hate the idea!"

"But it was your idea."

"It was a fake idea!"

Rosemary smiled.

"But Dylan, you're right. We should be embracing our schools. We shouldn't be living in our phones. We should be growing."

Growing. That word was really annoying me.

"Do you think we can have no contact for three weeks?" Rosemary asked, a glimmer in her eye.

"No, I don't! Absolutely not!" I practically shouted.

"You're funny."

"I'm not funny!"

Rosemary laughed. I didn't.

"It'll be an experiment. It's a challenge. You love challenges. You made the hockey team, and you never played hockey before."

"I only played hockey for you! And I was barely on the team. I was the fifth-string goalie. I was a human backboard in practice. I'd make an **ideal** archery range target!"

Rosemary laughed again. Yeah, I was making jokes, so she wouldn't think I was needy.

"We can do this," Rosemary said. "Are you with me?"

"No, no way," I thought to myself.

But I didn't feel like I had a choice. Yeah, Rosemary called the shots, and I'd started the ball rolling by lying to my parents. I'd brought this on. Reluctantly, I nodded.

"That's why I love you. You're up for anything."

*

When I was a kid, my parents attempted to transform me into the next Michael Phelps, the underwater version. Let me explain: I was a decent swimmer, but I was awesome at swimming underwater. Unfortunately, the Olympics don't have underwater swimming and aren't planning on adding it anytime soon, so my parents eventually surrendered their dream.

However, my underwater swimming exploits weren't a complete waste.

A swim coach noticed how loudly my parents encouraged me. When I was underwater, I could actually hear them. She suggested that we compete in the National Hollering Championships in Spivey's Corner, North Carolina. As I think about it now, the coach was probably goofing. Anyway, my parents passed on the idea at first, but then they had a change of heart. The championships were held during summer break, and my parents were probably bored. *The Castleton Chronicle* wrote a brief article about our experience. Here's a portion:

> Castleton's own, the Mills family, Jacob, Dana, and Dylan, finished in fourth place in the family division of the National Hollering Championships in Spivey's Corner, North Carolina. One of thirty-two families competing, the Mills family hollered Barry Manilow's "Copacabana" in front of a crowd of approximately 1,750. "We're disappointed but proud," said Mr. Mills, who along with his wife, Dana, are teachers at Castleton Middle School. Their son, Dylan, is in the third grade at Castleton Elementary. "We don't think of ourselves as loud people. However, we are easily excitable."
>
> "We'll be back next year, and we won't be denied," added Mrs. Mills.

We never did return though. After the championships, my father got a sore throat, and our doctor recommended no more prolonged hollering.

After quitting underwater swimming, I retired from athletics—until I went out for goalie. Of course, I didn't want to be a goalie, but I did want to spend time with Rosemary, the team's manager. Anyway, a deal was struck: Rosemary agreed to train me on the condition that I share with her my underwater swimming secrets. I have no idea why she wanted to swim underwater, and I didn't ask. We'd hang, and that's all that mattered.

Hockey training started with some brutal strength and cardio drills. After a hundred or so squats holding a medicine ball, we sprinted up and down Castleton Hill until we were drenched, and I was ready to quit.

Rosemary wouldn't let me.

"Oh, no! You got me into this, Mills. We're going to see this through!"

After a week, Rosemary's drills became more manageable, which meant I didn't feel like I was going to hurl. After a few days, Rosemary declared, "You're ready to face shots!"

I wasn't ready to face shots. Working out with Rosemary was going just fine. It was quality time.

"We'll start in my driveway," Rosemary commanded.

Rosemary still had a hockey goal from her playing days, as well as plenty of sticks, pucks, and pads, but she didn't have a goalie glove or a mask, so I used one of her old softball gloves and her mother's fencing mask. I looked ridiculous, but Rosemary didn't crack a smile. She wound up and started slapping shots at me—and past me. Rosemary looked like she could've starred on the Castleton varsity—the boy's varsity, which was always in contention for the state championship. I was in way over my head.

"Keep your nose on the puck!" Rosemary ordered. "All you care about in the world is stopping the puck. Concentrate!"

I did as I was told and repeated this mantra to myself: *Eyes on the puck. Prove that you don't suck!*

Yeah, I liked the way that sounded.

Eventually, I made a stop. And then another. And so on. After an hour—okay, twenty-two minutes—I was soaked, and my legs were burning. I was also careless. When Rosemary slapped a shot toward my midsection, my glove arrived late, and the puck slammed me just below my abdomen, in the worst possible place, which was not padded. I didn't immediately fall to the pavement in pain. I was running on fumes.

"Are you okay?" Rosemary asked.

"I'm fine," I replied through gritted teeth.

"I didn't get you there, did I?" Rosemary asked.

"No, you didn't get me there."

Yeah, she got me there.

As I strolled into Luncheonette for my shift, I was in a happy place. I don't know what I was meant to be, but it wasn't an athlete. I do, however, think I was meant to work at Luncheonette. I love it. I love being responsible and having a job. I love Luncheonette's pumpkin cinnamon pancakes and white chocolate chip cookies. I love how customers get all bent out of shape if we run out of almond milk.

But—and this is a huge but—I also hate Luncheonette.

Luncheonette is Castleton's epicenter for college chatter. Luncheonette: The name is misleading. Luncheonette is not a luncheonette. It's ritzy. But Castleton likes the concept of casual. Perhaps it makes the Luncheonette regulars feel like they're in a red state for a few hours. Its tables are marble, the silverware is actual silver, and the striped cushioned chairs are handwoven. The omelets look perfect, like something you would want to lay your head on rather than devour. Rosemary's favorite is the truffles and gruyere. I prefer Luncheonette's pumpkin cinnamon pancakes, which taste like the best candy, except they're somehow good for you, supposedly. I don't know how they do it, but Luncheonette bakes all its bread in house. My job is great for a kid, excellent money. I see and hear a lot, which is both good and bad.

As far as talking nonstop about college, the parents are worse than the kids, and the kids are a nightmare. Mr. Zelman—everyone calls him Mr. Z—is Castleton's worst offender. Currently, he has three children at elite *it* schools, and he has a five-year-old, Lil' Z, whom he's grooming. Mr. Z does something in finance. Just about everyone in Castleton does something in finance and is loaded—except my family. Yeah, my parents are middle school teachers, and we live on the very edge of Castleton—the wrong section, which consists of one block—*my* block. It was considered such a blight that there once was a small movement to redraw the village lines and move our block to the neighboring town.

Mr. Z is solidly built, broad, and noticeably short. Like just about everyone in Castleton, he's flawless in appearance. Mr. Z often goes from table to table at Luncheonette, asking kids in his unmistakable, high-pitched voice about their college plans. This compact man has approached kids as young as six years old. Mr. Z is always accompanied by his wife, Mrs. Z, a tall, slender woman with an immense nose that dominates her face. Mrs. Z doesn't say much. However, she is the most expressive person in Castleton. If someone mentions a school that she's really into—an *it* school of course—she'll smile widely, clasp her hands, and nod enthusiastically. If she's lukewarm on a school, she'll attempt a smile but fail miserably. When Mr. and Mrs. Z depart, they often discuss their findings in the parking lot. Luncheonette has enormous, magnificent windows, and I can watch their show. The rumor is that Mr. and Mrs. Z have separate bedrooms, and the joke is that Mrs. Z needs a separate bed for her ample nose. Yeah, there are some meanies in Castleton.

In the college hysteria department, Mr. and Mrs. Z are two of the worst offenders, but there are plenty of others.

Even the people I like get caught up in the insanity. Dorian Randolph, whom I've known since preschool, is my best friend. She went to boarding school for most of high school but returned home when her mother passed away. Dorian's father, Mr. Randolph, often fretted to me about Dorian's abundance of *it* college options. If it were anyone else, I would've been annoyed, but Mr. Randolph is hilarious, most of the time. Whenever Mr. Randolph felt he had gone on a bit longer than appropriate about the college stuff, he'd stop himself and say sarcastically, "These are white people's problems. I'm having a white person's problem!" And then he'd laugh at himself. Whenever Mr. Randolph would say "white people's problems," Luncheonette would come to an abrupt halt. After Mr. Randolph laughed, Luncheonette would return to normal. In Castleton, racism is just plain tacky, and being tacky is worse than being racist in Castleton. If anyone mentioned "white people's problems," it would raise eyebrows, but it gets way more attention when Mr. Randolph says it because he's black.

I try to avoid mentioning North South. But when I do, people either abruptly change the subject, quickly excuse themselves, or become confused. No one in Castleton knows much about North South—and they don't want to know. If it comes up in conversation—and it rarely does—it's dismissed as a party school, a punch line, a haven for fools, pretenders, and everything in between. If I'm asked about the name, I feign ignorance. But I know the truth. Maybe fifty years ago, North South was two community colleges: North and South. They combined so they could become a fully accredited, four-year school. If I were ever to explain this union, the Luncheonette crowd would get stuck on the school's community college beginnings, and the dining room would become a chamber of scattered, horrified murmurs.

- Underwater swimming stifled Dylan's development.
- He never made it to Mars because his head was in the clouds.
- Make sure you give the poor thing a nice tip.
- Is that a safety school for a safety school?

Yeah, in Castleton, I was a cautionary tale. I couldn't get out of this village fast enough.

SEPTEMBER

I was escaping. As planned, Dorian showed up with her Range Rover at dawn. Like just about everyone else in Castleton, Dorian had beaucoup bucks. Just to be sure that my parents didn't spot her, she parked a few houses down the street. I snuck out quietly through the side door. My mother would still be sleeping for at least another half hour—hopefully.

"Are you sure you want to do this?" Dorian asked as she helped me carry my duffel and trunk, which I'd painted with a montage. An art teacher once mentioned during a parent–teacher conference that I showed great potential with watercolors. Unfortunately, potential doesn't necessarily mean talent.

"Yes, it's easier this way for everyone," I explained. "I left a note for my mother. She'll tell my father." In case you're wondering, here it is:

> Mother Mills:
>   Good news! I got a ride up to North South. You won't have to drive, and you can enjoy the rest of your summer vacation. I'll call when I land, first thing. Promise.
>   Love,
>   Dylan

It was another necessary lie.

My parents swore they wanted to drive me up to North South, but I knew better. We all knew better. We might not even survive. With the methodical way my parents drive, the trip would take about seven and a half hours each way as opposed to the expected five and a half, and it wouldn't be pleasant. We'd be driving to my future, but the ride would be a playback of the past. If they hadn't already played that card, there would be many threats of divorce. And, of course, worst of all, my parents would bring up Rosemary, whom I was trying to not think about every second.

And so I did what I had to do. This wasn't so simple because North South is in the middle of nowhere. And since I don't have a driver's license yet, of course, I don't have a car. And no airport is nearby. I had one option: the bus. Don't—do not—groan. The bus has its positives. You don't have to report two hours early. There are no runway delays, and it's cheap. It's the travel of carless lone wolves. It felt very appropriate. Of course, I couldn't tell my parents about my plan. Though they'd been complaining about the drive for weeks, they'd make me feel guilty about depriving them of "the experience."

Dorian stepped up to be my chaperone. We'd become especially tight during senior year. After Dorian was accepted to every it school she applied to, some anonymous, spineless joker wrote some gibberish on social media, implying that Dorian's multiple acceptances were because of her race. Dorian could teach the teachers at Castleton, and she had the transcript to back it up. As tough as Dorian is, she was understandably upset, and there were some rough moments. She didn't vent to her father because she didn't want to upset him. Instead, she came to me. I didn't say much of anything, but I listened.

At the bus terminal, Dorian helped with my trunk and duffel and stayed next to me in line as I waited to board.

"How'd you leave it with Rosemary?"

"I don't even want to get started on that."

"Sorry."

If I was going to tell anyone, it would be Dorian—and part of me needed to tell someone. I exhaled and said what I didn't want to say: "Rosemary doesn't want to limit herself. She wants to grow."

"Grow?" Dorian interrupted. "Is this girl a plant? Is this as bad as it sounds?"

"We're free to see other people, but we're not breaking up."

"You're free to see other people, but you're not breaking up?"

"Exactly."

"How are you with all this?"

"I'm just peachy."

"Peachy, huh?"

"I'm fine," I sighed, attempting to front. "And another thing: We're not going to have any contact for the first three weeks of school."

"Who came up with that dumb idea?"

By my embarrassed expression, Dorian knew I was the culprit.

"It's a long story." It wasn't.

"Well, I will call you every day. I'm going to miss you."

"I'm going to miss you too." We embraced for a long moment. I tried not to get teary but failed.

"Hey pal, we're leaving," yelled the driver. "Say goodbye to your girlfriend and get on the bus!"

I took a window seat in the back and watched Dorian watch me. As the bus engine started, I needed to move, to do something drastic. I abruptly got out of my seat and started walking toward the driver. We weren't out of the terminal. There was still time to escape my escape. I didn't want to do this. I didn't want to go to North South. No, no no! I did not want to grow!

It was all a mistake.

But as quickly as I'd gotten up, I did a 180 and sat back down. I had to go to North South. Castleton wasn't Castleton anymore. Rosemary wasn't there. My parents were divorced. Yeah, I still can't believe that. And I wasn't a high school student. I was barely a high school student when I *was* a high school student—but now I was really not a high school student.

I wasn't bailing on North South.

My bus left on time and everything moved along. There was no traffic, and I settled in for the haul. My bus was relatively empty, just me and the friends and family of prisoners. Yeah, prisoners. North South is about twenty-five miles away from a prison. When there was a well-publicized prison break not too long ago, a rumor circulated that the escaped prisoners were hiding out at North South, perhaps even posing as students or professors. If you've heard of North South, there's a good chance it's because of the prison break news coverage. The escapees were on the run for at least two weeks. I think some of the North South students assisted with the search.

Everyone on the bus kept to themselves. I studied my phone, hit the wrong button, and Rosemary's Instagram popped up.

And there she was.

I couldn't turn away. Rosemary was already on her *it* campus, and she was smiling in front of a gothic building. Rosemary looked magnificent. Her bronze hair was glowing more than usual, she was tan, and her teeth were perfect. And her eyes. . . . In this pic, they looked turquoise. Since she arrived at her *it* school, Rosemary was looking even better. I guess *it* schools do that.

Almost impossible to believe now but Rosemary wasn't always the magnificent shiny specimen. After she tore her ACL for the second time and quit hockey, Rosemary hit a rut. She lost her athletic physique and kept her hair in a bun, always.

Maybe three hours into my journey, my phone rang. I didn't want to talk to anyone, not even Dorian, well, maybe Dorian.

Yeah, I was missing Rosemary.

But I had to take this. I was feeling guilty. I was guilty.

"Hello."

"Where are you?" my parents shouted in unison. They were together again, on speaker. You're divorced. Why don't you act like it?

"Did you get my note?"

"I didn't get a note!" my father grumbled.

"I figured Mom would tell you."

"You should've sent me a note. It's insensitive, Dylan."

"I apologize."

"Well, where are you? Could you at least tell me *that*?" asked my father.

"I don't know where I am." Wrong answer.

"You don't know where you are?" yelled my father.

"I'm on the highway. I'm in the middle of nowhere." I looked out the window to nothing but trees. "It's very rural. There are no signs."

"Do you want us to come up?" asked my mother.

Instantly, I imagined my parents rescuing me and returning me to Castleton. I quickly reminded myself that Castleton wasn't Castleton.

"It's okay. It's easier this way. Why should you be on the road for fifteen hours? But thank you." My parents were silenced. They didn't want to be on the road for fifteen minutes.

"Is it safe?" my father asked.

"Yes, the bus is very safe. When's the last time you heard of terrorists hijacking a bus? And it's better for the environment."

Until this very moment, I hadn't expressed any such concern. Abruptly the bus pulled over.

"Phone conversations are prohibited!" announced the bus driver over the loudspeaker. "If you don't follow the rules, you'll have to get off at the next stop."

My parents heard the message loud and clear.

"Well, you better go then," directed my mother, restraining a faint sniffle. "You know best."

"I'll call when I land," I promised. "I love you."

I meant it.

*

"Lewisville!" announced the bus driver over the intercom. We'd arrived at the prison stop. Weary loved ones gathered their belongings and trudged off, leaving me alone with the driver. I imagined Rosemary visiting me in prison—and then I stopped myself.

Why on earth would I be in prison?

Thirty-five minutes later, it was my turn.

"You're up kid!" yelled the driver. "You can call your girlfriend now."

"No, I can't," I thought to myself.

North South is in the town of North South. When the college was renamed, the town renamed itself.

"They're not too quick up there," I imagined Mr. Z remarking. "They gotta make things simple—one-stop shopping!"

I was out of Castleton, but yeah, Castleton was still in me.

I sat on my trunk on the sidewalk. It was chilly, at least twenty degrees colder than Castleton. I'd never visited North South because I hadn't planned on coming. Until the very last moment, I held out hope that Ms. Davenport's school, a wannabe *it* school, would come to its senses and pluck me off their waiting list. Even though I knew I shouldn't, I pulled out Ms. Davenport's letter, which I kept close to me at all times.

> Dear Mr. Mills:
> Thank you for your patience. This year, we've had a highly competitive applicant pool, our largest ever in fact. While you have done some fine work, I'm sorry to inform you that we do not have a place for you in our incoming freshman class. We appreciate your interest and wish you the best in your future endeavors.
> Sincerely,
> Marcia Davenport

Reading this did what it always did: It reminded me that I came up short. I didn't know much about Ms. Davenport's school, other than it was considered respectable by Castleton's ridiculous standards. "It's an up-and-comer," I imagined Mr. Z saying. As much as I wanted to, I couldn't keep myself from dissecting every word of Ms. Davenport's rejection letter. What do you mean "patient"? I've been impatient. How many times did I badger your office? And you're wishing me the best? No, you're telling me to get lost.

I ordered myself to get a grip. Of course, I'd ordered myself to get a grip many times before, but it seemed to never work. This time though, it was different. I was alone in a strange place. If I hadn't had that bad experience with the gummy bears, I'd smoke some dope. Maybe that would calm me. You might be wondering about those bad-ass gummy bears. We were at the Castle, and, as usual, I didn't want to be there. Anyway, everyone was doing them, and I didn't want to seem like a tool. I had a few red ones, and almost immediately, I started to feel off. Soon, the nausea set in, and I sprinted toward the river. Somehow, I kept it down until I got out of everyone's sight. At least I thought I was. When I came up for air, Rosemary was by my side with a water bottle.

"Everything's going to be fine," she told me repeatedly.

"I sure hope so," I finally managed. "I don't want to be the first person who OD'd on gummy bears."

Rosemary laughed so hard, I thought she might hurl. Eventually, I started to laugh too.

I was back in a happy place, for a few moments.

North South was dead. It was late afternoon, and everything was shut down. My dormitory, which was named the North Pole—I kid you not—wasn't far, less than a mile away, according to my phone. My trunk and duffel made walking it impossible. An Uber wasn't available for at least forty-five minutes. In Castleton, it was instant service, eight minutes at most.

As I considered my options, I took in the immense mountains. They were magnificent, but they made me feel small and even more alone. Besides my two weeks at space camp, I'd never been away from home. In my sheltered village, I was sheltered. It was still hard to fathom that I wouldn't be working at Luncheonette. And then, of course, there was Rosemary. I was trying to not count the seconds. As I contemplated this, I started doing what I do: stringing words together.

> I'm lost in the trees.
> When are you going to come back to me?

As I repeated the words, a beat-up pickup truck pulled over. Two tough big guys were in the truck. They looked like they'd just broken out of Lewisville. For all I know, they had.

"What are you doing?" asked the driver, accusingly. His hair was unkempt, his face scruffy. He was accompanied by an enormous, muscular tattooed man in the passenger seat.

"You need a ride?" he asked gruffly.

For a moment, I didn't reply. I was stuck on this fact, which I'm embarrassed to admit: I'd never spoken to a man, or woman for that matter, in overalls.

Castleton didn't do overalls.

"Do you need a ride, pal?" Pal implies friend, something these guys would never be.

"I'm waiting for an Uber."

"Uber Goober! Why wait? We'll drive you now." When I hesitated, he became angry. "What is it? Do you think you're better than us?"

"No," I stammered. "I'm just waiting for an Uber, like I said before."

"Like you said before? Who do you think you are, college kid?"

"I don't think I'm anyone," I said softly.

What did I just say? "I don't think I'm anyone" had a nice feel. But my pals didn't seem to pick up on that. They just stared at me with a dead-eyed stare.

I was scared. How do I make these guys go away?

"We'll give you a ride for $20 . . . make it $25!"

A second later, a much nicer black truck pulled over. It was emblazoned with North South's unique logo: North South was spelled out in caps. An arrow pointing up was in front of the N and an arrow pointing down was in front of the S. It was North South security to the rescue, finally.

"Good evening, gentleman," said the man in the North South truck. "How's everyone doing?"

"We found him sitting here on the sidewalk," said the driver.

The man in the truck got out. In his dark North South fleece and khakis, he didn't look like security. He was boyishly handsome, tall, and athletic with light brown hair. If he was in North South's catalog, I missed him. I'd just glanced at North South's catalog, which was more like a pamphlet, at least compared to Rosemary's *it* school's, where the students were annoyingly photogenic. I wouldn't be surprised if they hired models to pose as their students. This man would fit right in at Rosemary's *it* school. For a moment, the man studied me before his face curled into a smile.

"Dylan Mills?" he said after a moment.

"How'd you know?"

"I'm Mr. Wells. I'm North South's president. I recognized you from your application. It was unforgettable, very well done."

I had written about my experiences as the fifth-string goalie and included images, video, and even some artwork— well, watercolor paintings. I guess that counts as art.

"Thank you. I'm glad someone read it."

Why'd I say that? Of course someone read it. By suggesting someone hadn't, I was implying that North South's admissions office didn't read their applications.

"They don't," I imagined Mr. Z howling. "They'll take anyone!"

"It was passed on to me. It was very funny. I think most of the faculty read it. We're excited to have you."

"Someone's excited to have you!" Mr. Z screamed. "You better stay put!"

Why do I keep hearing his annoying voice?

"I'm glad to be here."

I was glad that he was rescuing me from these goons— whoever they were.

"Well thank you, gentleman," Mr. Wells said to the two men. "We appreciate. I'll take it from here. Have a pleasant evening." Mr. Wells was good. He was telling the men to have a nice night and to get lost.

"Can I give you a ride to the North Pole?" Mr. Wells offered.

"We didn't know if you were going to show or what," said Mr. Wells when we were in his truck. I said it before, this guy was good. He knew exactly where my head was at. "You didn't register for classes. The final, final deadline was the end of the day yesterday."

"Final, final deadline?"

North South had sent me a steady stream of emails over the summer, but I'd only glanced at them. Yeah, I'd been bad. I'd been counting on Ms. Davenport.

"Three days before that, we had the final deadline," Mr. Wells explained.

There was hope. I just might be saved from North South after all. I'd missed the final, final deadline. Even if I wanted to, I couldn't enroll. It was an administrative error. I'd be forced to return to Castleton. I'd work at Luncheonette, save up, and take a class or two somewhere, maybe. And then I'd reset. Reset! I liked how that sounded. Where would I go? Would I even go anywhere? Why did I have to go to college? Maybe I'd go to culinary school, even though I didn't particularly love cooking. I loved eating though, so maybe I could make it work. Or maybe, I'd get a job near Rosemary's *it* school. I'd work in a restaurant. Or maybe I'd open my own restaurant with all the college money I wouldn't be spending. I wouldn't have to cook. I'd direct and manage. Our specialty would be pumpkin cinnamon pancakes. It was guaranteed success. Rosemary would bring all her friends in between classes. After she graduated, we'd—

And then, abruptly, my fantasy vanished.

"I registered for you," said Mr. Wells. "Just in case."

"Well, thank you," I managed. "I'm so glad."

*

I didn't want it, and I definitely didn't ask for it, but Mr. Wells insisted on taking me on a quick campus tour. North South's campus was a confusing hodgepodge of buildings. Right next to a magnificent lake on the edge of campus was a palatial solar-heated barn. Perhaps North South's most recognizable building was its colonial-style chapel, located at its center. It had steep white steps and a bell tower. It could fit right in at any *it* school. The chapel was no longer in use though, and its single room was used for storage. Not far from the chapel was a statue of a short rotund man. North South's most generous benefactor was an alum and the long-time singer for a world-famous band, known as much for their fanatic, hippie fans as their music. He'd left a substantial gift to North South, and because of him, North South was going through an extensive makeover.

"You came to North South at just the right time," Mr. Wells explained energetically.

North South was in the midst of completing a modern state-of-the-art student center. It was open for students, but construction crews were still on-site completing the job. On the edge of the campus was a beat-up, parked van. Mr. Wells explained that the van was a longtime campus staple and served amazing hummus. North South was impeccably clean, well maintained, and scenic. It also smelled good— for the most part. When we went by the solar-heated barn, I got a strong whiff of manure, which immediately made me think of Castleton, though I never smelled manure in Castleton.

"You don't have an equestrian team, do you?" I asked.

"No, we don't. Are you an equestrian?"

"No," I mumbled.

I was too embarrassed to mention that Castleton had an equestrian team. I also felt stupid for presuming that the North South campus would be a dump. It was actually quite impressive.

As I walked up the stairs to my room on the fourth floor, the reality hit me: I'm going to be sharing a room.

I didn't want to share a room.

I hadn't shared a room since space camp, and things hadn't gone well. My roommate was an arrogant kid who thought he was headed to Jupiter. The kids at space camp were smart but no fun. Not surprising when you think about it: They were obsessed with getting away from Earth.

Who would I be sharing a room with? Would he wear overalls and chew tobacco like the guys in the truck? Would he be out on parole? I scanned my North South email for my roommate's identity but couldn't locate it. Well, I'd find out soon enough.

On my floor, I heard the faint sounds of heavy metal from the end of the hallway. Not a peep was coming from my room though, and my door was shut. I knocked a few times. Nothing. I didn't want to walk in on my new roommate at a, uh, bad time. I quickly put my ear against the door, still nothing. He probably wasn't there. I turned the knob, but the door was locked. I inserted my room card, and I walked in but didn't get far.

It wasn't a room.

It was a closet with a single bed, a desk, and a dresser. It was a single. I was fortunate that I hadn't brought much. There was nowhere to put it. I lay down on the bare mattress.

After a few minutes, my stomach growled. I walked over to the cafeteria, but it was closed. With no other options, I went to the idle van. A sign posted on the van's side read "Legend in His Own Mind: Quarters Presents the Van Café." Where was the café in this setup? I'm embarrassed to admit this, but I'd never eaten at a food truck before. They were illegal in Castleton. And even if they weren't, I don't think they'd go over too well. No, Castleton was not a food truck kind of village. And I could understand why. It just didn't feel sanitary. I was having second thoughts about eating from a food truck now, but I was starved. On a chalkboard just outside the truck was a menu with one item in capital letters: HUMMUS! A man with shoulder-length light brown hair, wrapped in a white bandana, in a tie-dyed shirt, sat in the passenger seat. He looked like a student, a forty-five-year-old student. His eyes were shut. When I got within a few yards though, his eyes popped open wide.

What was this man on? I doubt gummy bears.

"What's uppp?" he said excitedly. "What's uppp? What's uppp? First year, huh?"

Was I wearing a sign?

"First hour," I replied.

"First hour of the best four years of your life. What can I do you for?" This burnout wasn't wearing gloves. I was out of here!

"You know I'm gonna take a rain check," I told him.

"My man, no can do. I don't write checks and there's no rain in the forecast," he grinned. "Don't you want to eat? Yes, you do. Everyone wants to eat!"

I went for it and ordered what Mr. Wells suggested, and Quarters scurried into his vessel. When he returned, he handed me a heaping plate of hummus, carrots, and pita, which was topped with Tabasco and oregano in a Styrofoam tray. And yeah, he had put plastic gloves on.

"Enjoy! And enjoy North South. I'm in my twenty-fifth year. I showed up freshman year, and I've never left. There's no better place on earth. I'm Quarters. What's your name?"

"Dylan."

"Like the singer. Welcome amigo."

I took my hearty plate back to my closet. Even though it looked amazing, I was still a little skeptical. After working at Luncheonette, I'd become a food snob.

"That burnout probably dropped some acid in it!" I imagined Mr. Z bellowing.

I forced myself to take a bite, slowly. Just as Mr. Wells had promised, the hummus was delicious—Luncheonette quality, well, almost. After devouring it way too quickly, I closed my eyes. I promised that I'd do so for just a minute or two, but it turned into five. And then I was gone.

A persistent, aggressive knock at the door throttled me awake. Who could it be? It was after midnight. Wrong door. I wouldn't answer.

"Is anyone home?" asked the person knocking. "It's your RA!"

"What's an RA?" I asked.

"Resident adviser."

It sounded like a position at a psychiatric institution.

When I opened my door, a tall man in boxers and a T-shirt was staring directly at me. His hair was sticking out in fifteen different directions, and he was annoyed. My RA explained that my parents had contacted campus security who had contacted him. My parents were concerned that they hadn't heard from me. I apologized profusely and explained that I'd meant to call but passed out in a hummus coma. My RA didn't want to hear it.

"Call your parents!" he ordered before walking away in a huff. I grabbed my phone. I'd accidentally turned the ringer off. I had a million messages.

Rosemary.

She had decided to break our three-week hiatus. I knew she couldn't hold out. I couldn't hold out. I was needy.

But every message was from my parents. I left a voice mail for my mother, informed her that everything was fine. Just in case, I also texted. I didn't want to see my angry RA again.

Mother Mills:

I'm here at North South! All's well. Sorry I didn't call. I ate an enormous dinner of hummus, and it was great, but it knocked me out. Miss you. I'll call tomorrow first thing.

P.S. Please don't contact campus security again. Much appreciate.

Before I hit send, I deleted the P.S. If I told my parents to not do something, they'd do the opposite. They had a standard, succinct explanation: "We're your parents!"

"I get it," I'd tell my father. "But . . ."

"No buts!" he'd say with a grin. "We know we're annoying. It's our job."

As I lay in bed, I pondered how I wound up at North South in the first place. I remembered my guidance counselor touting it as a diamond in the rough with an elite fine arts department. I also reminded myself that North South was public and was the right price—practically free, at least compared to some of these *it* schools—which was perfect for the Mills family because we weren't rolling in it. Castleton taxes were insane, and in short, we were tweeners as far as financial aid. We didn't make enough, but we made too little. Yeah, I had been accepted to other places—no *it* schools—but North South was as good as any of those, and I wouldn't wind up in debt. And during the application scramble, I had other things on my mind.

North South was just a name, an unknown name, on a list of schools, one of which I would attend in the future, something I didn't want to plan for. I wanted things to stay just the way they were. And no, I didn't want to grow under any circumstances.

*

I cringed when I saw geology, my science requirement, on my schedule. I wasn't sure what my forte was, but it wasn't geology. And I wasn't looking forward to sitting in class again. Who was I fooling? Maybe I didn't belong at school at all.

The big question: Where did I belong?

I went to the main office and picked up my North South ID. I wish my ears didn't stick out so much and that my freckles weren't so loud. I reminded myself of what my father always told me: Wishing is for fairy tales.

When I returned to the North Pole, some students were playing basketball on the court behind the dorm. I took a seat on the grass, not far away. I looked up at the mountains and imagined the escaped prisoners. If they were brought up in Castleton, things would've been different.

"You're in!" ordered a tall blond kid, who had one arm completely covered in tattoos. I should've sat further away. "We need a fifth."

"Thanks, but I'm not—"

"You're on our team. We're defending," ordered Tattoo Kid.

"Thanks, but I don't play basketball."

"Who doesn't play basketball?" he sneered.

"I have chronic irritable bowel syndrome that sets in when I run on concrete," I muttered.

"What did you say?"

"Nothing."

"Look, guy," said Tattoo Kid. "Man up!"

I didn't like being referred to as guy and ordered to man up. Was the implication that I wasn't a man? I'm not—at least not yet, but you know what I mean, I think. But I'd play so I could shut Tattoo Kid up, and then I'd never play basketball again, ever. I tied my almost new fluorescent running sneakers that my parents had gotten me and took the court. I gave myself a pep talk, well, kind of: Stay away from the ball! Unfortunately, Tattoo Kid acted as if we were competing in Game 7 of the NBA Finals. He was constantly shouting directions, and there wasn't a three-pointer he didn't take. When I did receive the ball a few times, I passed immediately. Fortunately, the person I was defending, the sole female on the court, had selfish teammates, and she didn't see the ball nearly as much as she deserved. She was exceptionally quick and an adept dribbler. It was as if she had the ball on a string. She wore baggy shorts; a nylon, sleeveless shirt, which showed off her lean, muscular arms; and a red bandana, which completely covered her hair. She was an athlete, and I was, well, a glee club dropout, retired fifth-string goalie. However, I was pleased that I wasn't embarrassing myself. Frustrated, understandably, with her number of touches, Red Bandana started breaking toward the offensive end of the court as soon as her team inbounded, and she scored two quick baskets.

"What are you doing?" Tattoo Kid yelled after the second. Even if I had a comeback, I couldn't get it out. I was hyperventilating. Red Bandana was quick. When Red Bandana sprinted down the court yet again, her teammate tossed her a three-quarters of the court lob. I went full speed, but she still had me by half a step. Just before the ball fell onto her fingertips, I leapt and managed to tip the ball. It hit Red Bandana on her shoulder and rolled out of bounds. Somehow though, my feet got tangled, and I wound up face down on the concrete. I think I lost consciousness for a second.

"You better take a break," ordered Tattoo Kid. For a moment I thought he was being nice, but then I noticed that there was another kid waiting to play.

After I got some rubbing alcohol and a bandage from the North Pole's main office for the scrape on my arm, I took a walk to Quarters's café. A few people were sitting on chairs.

"What happened to you, Pablo?" asked Quarters.

"Pickup basketball," I said glumly.

As Quarters prepared me one of his other specialties, a watermelon iced tea, I studied the collage of vertical disc team photos on his van's door, each placed inside a small frisbee. The photos went back to the mid-'90s, and Quarters seemed to be in every shot. He explained that vert disc was like frisbee golf on a mountain.

"Best sport ever invented," Quarters declared. "I'm biased. I invented it." Quarters, North South's vert disc coach, invited me to come out for preseason training, which started in a few weeks. "It's a lot more fun than tired basketball with a lot cooler people," Quarters promised. I wasn't interested. I was done with organized and disorganized sports.

I'd been at North South for more than twenty-four hours, and I still hadn't unpacked or made my bed. I just hadn't gotten around to it—yeah, my specialty. However, I wasn't all bad. I did get around to purchasing my textbooks. I looked through North South's pamphlet. There was a page on vert disc with a photo of Quarters. He was wearing a headband, and his hair was bleached blond. I picked up my geology textbook and stared at it. I told myself that this was a new chapter, and I must embrace it. I pledged to devour this geology and commit it to memory, but then I started the first chapter, and it tasted meh.

*

I knew I'd forgotten something. I just didn't know what. My phone said 5:04. Suddenly, it hit me. I was supposed to go on Mr. Wells's hike. I wasn't up for it, but I felt obligated—and guilty. Yeah, I'd already missed the final, final deadline. I'd already had a late-night visit from my RA. What else could I screw up?

I frantically ran downstairs to the North Pole's lounge. They hadn't left. It was only a handful of people. It wouldn't have been a big deal if I hadn't shown, but Mr. Wells was genuinely pleased to see me.

We walked around the lake and up a hiking trail, nothing too rigorous. No one was too cliquey either. As we walked, I wondered if Rosemary was also on a freshman hike she didn't want to be on. If she was, it wouldn't have been much of a hike, as her *it* school was overwhelmingly flat. We took a path to the edge of the forest, where there were a few benches and an *it*-school-worthy view. After we soaked it in, Mr. Wells invited us to sit.

"Welcome. Thank you for joining me on this short journey," Mr. Wells announced. "Of course this is the start of a longer journey, and I want us to get acquainted. I'd like everyone to say their name and something about themselves."

Quarters was in the group. How had I missed him?

"I'll start. I'm Mr. Wells. As you all know, I'm North South's president, and I have a secret," he grinned mischievously. "I had a C– average my freshman year."

I didn't see that coming.

"My name's Quarters, and I have a lot of secrets. I would've loved a C– average. Quarters isn't the name on my birth certificate."

I learned that Quarters had flunked out of North South at least twice, and he'd been expelled for driving his van into the lake. After three appeals, he was allowed to return— and never leave. After Quarters, everyone looked around nervously.

"I'm Dylan, ah, I've been to seven Barry Manilow concerts. You probably don't know who he is, but my parents think he's the greatest, and I'm into him too. He's very cool."

What was I saying? Barry might be great, but he's definitely not cool.

"I know Barry," replied a muscular kid with longish black hair. "He's awesome!"

"You know Barry?" I asked.

"Nah, I'm just messin'. But I had a dentist named Larry Mazlowe. I'll never forget him because he had these immense buck teeth," said the muscular kid smiling. Everyone laughed. "But now you got me curious about this Barry cat so I'm gonna check him out. . . . And my name's Walter, but everyone calls me Wally. I love fast motorcycles. I was born down the road at the prison in Lewisville. My mom was inside when she had me. I guess you could say I was born guilty, but please don't."

After Wally's very personal statement, everyone was silent for a moment, until the guy next to him spoke up.

"I'm Jimmy. Everyone calls me Jimmy," said a tall, thin guy confidently. He was dressed in all black, and he had shades on, even though the sun was no longer out. "I walk and whistle in my sleep, so if you see me walking around the North Pole in the middle of the night acting strange, help a fella out."

"Mary Lou," squeaked an awkward, tall, slender woman. "If you saw me two months ago, you wouldn't recognize me. I was three times this size. I just had gastric bypass surgery. My parents gave it to me as a graduation gift."

A bearded kid in hunting attire was next. "My name's Andre. I'd prefer not to say anything about myself. No offense."

"No offense taken," replied Mr. Wells.

"My name's Jackie. Last year, I was Jack. But on some days, I still feel like being called Jack. It's complicated."

After the final person spoke, Mr. Wells encouraged us to introduce ourselves to fellow students who didn't attend the hike.

As we walked back, I obsessed over my statement. I should've said something more substantial, or maybe I should've just pulled an Andre. He said nothing, but everyone thought it was funny and cool. Barry was Barry, a legend—but definitely *not* cool. But Wally didn't seem to care. He invited me to a post-hike gathering.

"We're in Room 420," said Wally, who was roomies with Jimmy. "It's BYS!"

"BYS?"

"Bring yourself!"

After a quick shower, I lay down on my still bare mattress. Mistake. I didn't want to get up. But I forced myself to rally. I must try. And it wasn't like I had to commute. Wally was on my floor. I would be at the gathering, if I could find it. I walked up and down my floor several times, but there was no Room 420. I must've misheard, or maybe it was a prank. Let's have some fun at the expense of the guy who likes Barry. As I walked back to my closet, dejected, I heard loud music coming from Room 402. I also smelled incense. At least, I think it was incense. Did Wally say 402 or 420? A guy and a girl in tie-dyed shirts walked past me, opened the door, and strolled right in. I followed. Room 402 was smoky, loud, and crowded. It was enormous compared to my closet. It was a double and lofts had been installed. I hadn't made my bed, and they already had lofts. They'd also soundproofed the room with foam and covered the walls with posters, all iconic musicians with the exception of four. Three were of iconic actresses: Rita Hayworth, Marilyn Monroe, and Raquel Welch. The fourth poster was odd but strangely familiar: a cattle rancher sitting atop a jackrabbit. Wally sat in the corner, smiling, holding bongos. Jimmy, who still had his shades on, was next to him holding his guitar.

"What up, duuude!" Wally greeted, half embracing me. North South had given the incoming freshman North South T-shirts, which were a jarring bright orange with the black North South logo. Wally had already removed the sleeves. If I had his biceps, I would've done the same. On the back was the number 26, our graduation year. I didn't plan on wearing mine.

"You said 420, right?" I asked.

"I did," replied Wally.

"You're in 402."

"We're unofficially 420. I thought everyone was in on it. It's a North Pole thing. My bad."

I learned later that April 20 is international Marijuana Day, which was news to me. Besides the potent gummy bears, I had no weed experience whatsoever. For kids who were into dope, North South was *it*. A magazine dedicated to marijuana use had selected North South as one of the best colleges in the country—for weed.

"Let me get something for you," Wally said, smiling. "We've got some beer and vodka. And we also have some coke."

"You have coke?" I asked in an agitated whisper.

"You're funny, duuude," Wally laughed. "We have coke—soda. It goes well with the vodka."

"I'll just have some coke. I'm not much of a drinker."

"Whatever you say, duuude."

In fewer than fifteen seconds, Wally'd referred to me as duuude three times. Suddenly, my life flashed before my eyes. I imagined Wally and me in a nursing home in wheelchairs.

"Duuude," Wally asked. "You wanna race?"

I took a seat on the only available space, on a corner of the couch, which was underneath one of the lofts, next to the overly affectionate couple in tie-dyed T-shirts, who seemed identical in every way, including their dandruff. I ordered myself not to stare at them, but I didn't listen to myself, no, not the first time. It was uncomfortable. I'm no fan of PDA, and worse, they made me think of Rosemary.

Abruptly, Jimmy launched into a guitar solo, and Wally started to sing, well, kind of. It was a wail. I made out the lyrics. I think. Anyway, he had my attention, and I finally stopped staring at Dandruff Duo.

Will I learn anything?
Safety School!
Is it worth it?
Safety School!
Am I wasting my time?
Safety School!
Don't know what I wanna be.
Safety School!

What Wally lacked in vocal abilities, he made up in sheer presence. As Wally wailed, he nodded furiously and hopped frantically across the room. After the third verse, he tore off what remained of his North South T-shirt, and everyone cheered. Even Dandruff Duo came up for air.

I need that degree to be well.
Safety School!
I need that degree, or I'll go to hell.
Safety School!
Safety School!
Safety School!

Wally held out his hand to us as if it were a microphone and signaled for us to repeat the chorus, and we did.

Everyone was yelling, including me. I was yelling to Mr. and Mrs. Z and all the Castleton meanies. I was also yelling at myself. After the song, the Dandruff Duo exited, and a perspiring Wally collapsed on the couch next to me.

"Whose song is that?" I asked.

"It's mine, I guess. I was just goofing around."

"Does it have a name?"

"Nope, not yet."

"How 'bout 'Safety School'?"

"Why would I call it that?"

"Well, the chorus."

"'Satan's School' is the chorus."

Yeah, I'd misheard the lyrics. I was embarrassed again.

"I thought you were singing something else."

"What?"

"Safety school."

"Why would I sing that?"

"I don't know. Maybe this was your safety school."

"No way. North South was my reach."

"You're a Neanderthal!" I heard Mr. Z scream. Yeah, he was referring to me.

Minutes later, 420 was empty. Even with the soundproofing, our beleaguered RA had given us two warnings about excessive noise. He said that a third would mean "severe consequences." Getting expelled before school started. Yeah, I could live with that. I'd return to Castleton and then, well . . . I wasn't quite sure. Everyone else, however, didn't want severe consequences, so everyone scattered. There was no more coke anyway. It'd been fun, and I returned to my closet, exhilarated. I was going to dive back into geology, maybe. But before I could insert my security card in my door, I was blocked by a hand.

"Duuude, what are you doing?" asked Wally with a serious expression, still shirtless.

"I'm turning in."

"You're what?"

"I figured that the party was over," I replied defensively.

"That was the pre-party. School's about to begin, my friend."

"What'd you just say?"

"I don't know. What did I say?"

"Just repeat your last sentence."

"What did I say?"

"No, before that."

"I don't know."

"Before that?"

"Okay, let me concentrate." Wally closed his eyes and pointed each of his index fingers on his temples. "Okay, I think I got it. . . . School's about to begin, my friend."

Yeah, I had my first friend at North South.

There was good reason to party, finally.

*

Wally, Jimmy, and I attacked the monstrous half mountain to get to the town of North South and Fat Nancy's, one of North South's most well-known nightspots, which I'd never heard of until moments ago. I'd learn later that the bar's proprietor, Nancy, was rail thin. When we got within shouting distance, my anxiety reappeared. My procrastination had caught up with me, again.

"I got a problem," I said nervously. "I don't have a driver's license."

"You lost it?" Jimmy asked.

"Never got one."

"How could you never get one?"

"I don't drive."

"Why not?"

"I could bike anywhere in my village, and I just never got around to it."

"Village?" Wally raised brow. "Duuude!"

"It's a long story."

"No worries," Jimmy said as he swiftly reached into his wallet and handed me a license with his photo. "Use this," he said. "It's my fake." Jimmy also handed me the black knit hat he'd been wearing. "Put this on." I took it but hesitated to put it on, and Jimmy sensed my apprehension. "They're not looking, and you're of age, so what's the harm?"

"And you're not even drinking," Wally added. "You can have as much coke as you like."

I put on Jimmy's hat and quickly memorized the details on his fake ID. I wasn't sold on the plan. Jimmy and I didn't look alike. He was dark. I was orange. I wanted to be allowed into Fat Nancy's, but I didn't want to be the odd man out on my first night out. Even more than that though, I didn't want any problems with law enforcement. Was this the beginning of a long downward spiral that would wind up with me in prison? I tried to be optimistic. It was dark out, and the hat was a good disguise. I changed the subject.

"Do you really walk and whistle in your sleep?" I asked Jimmy.

"Nah, I just didn't know what else to say. I never know what to say at those things. I wouldn't have even gone if Wally hadn't dragged me. Did you really go to seven Barry Manilow concerts?"

"I actually went to eleven. I miscounted."

Just as we got to the front of the line, the bouncer's flashlight batteries went dead. He barely looked at our IDs, then waved us in. We descended a long, dim, narrow staircase. The music, which I can best describe as punk country, was cranked. After turning a sharp corner at the bottom of the stairs, we entered a dark, congested, smoke-filled rectangle, lit up by several scattered fluorescent lights. Fat Nancy's was packed, and everyone was having a blast. About thirty-five people, who ran the gamut in ages, enthusiastically danced in the middle of the room. One woman in a round black hat, who was probably old enough to be my grandmother, was the most enthusiastic. Each time she poked out her hand, she wiggled her fingers. Almost immediately, Wally started talking to a woman. Meanwhile, Jimmy had disappeared. I found some space by one of the walls, which was covered by frisbees, just like the ones at Quarters's café. Each had a year and the team's record. "National Champions" was written on a few.

"Are you drinking?" asked a girl with short, peroxide-blond hair. At least I think that's what she said. It was loud in there. She was about a foot shorter than me, but she had a lean, powerful build.

"Excuse me?" I replied.

"Nope," she replied with a smile. "No excuses allowed."

"Are you drinking?" she asked.

"I'm not." I must've had a confused expression on my face.

"You don't know who I am, do you?" I didn't.

"I'm sorry."

"You should be. You were on me today."

I was *on* her today? What was she talking about?

"We were playing basketball behind the North Pole. I'm Sam."

Without her red bandana, I hadn't recognized her.

"Correction: I was failing to cover you."

Sam laughed.

"How's your arm?"

"I'll live."

"I know you'll live, but how's your arm?"

"It's nothing, but thanks for asking."

"No problem. So why aren't you drinking?"

"I don't know." But I did. I didn't really drink.

"Well, do you mind if I corrupt you . . . just a little?" Before I could reply, Sam pressed the large mason glass she'd been holding, with murky liquid, to my lips.

"Try this. It'll change your life. . . . Well, not really, but it tastes good." After the walk uptown, I was thirsty. I was in college. I was of age. Why not? There were no Luncheonette shifts to prepare for. I took a sip. It did taste good—fruit punch with a bite. Instantly, I felt calmer, and immediately, I wanted another.

"Tasty, huh?"

"Yeah. What is it?"

"They call it Fat Nancy's Special Blend. They won't reveal the ingredients. You can share mine." I hesitated for a moment, before taking another sip and then another.

And another.

What was I doing? Was this seeing other people? No, it was just sipping a fellow classmate's drink. But if I was seeing other people, what was wrong with that? Isn't that what Rosemary wanted? We continued to sip and watch the dance floor. Now the woman with the black hat was standing in one place, poking her head back and forth like a peacock. Wally was smiling, dancing with everyone and no one, which is what everyone was basically doing. When the Special Blend was gone, we headed over to the bar across the room, passing Wally. I wasn't going to interrupt him, but he stopped me.

"Who's Blondie?" Wally whispered excitedly.

"She let me drink her Special Blend. Awesome hoops player."

"I thought you didn't drink!"

I rolled my eyes and changed the subject. "Who's that girl you were dancing with earlier?"

"Duuude, that's no girl. She's my mother's parole officer."

I never knew someone whose parent had a parole officer, until now. I guess I was broadening my horizons. Wally returned to dancing, and I returned to the sidelines with Sam. I had my own Special Blend now.

"You know that guy?" Sam asked.

"We just met today on the orientation hike, but it feels like we've known each other our entire lives. . . . I feel like I've known you my entire life."

Yeah, the Special Blend had already taken full effect. I was a little light-headed, well, probably a lot more than a little. I wasn't even a lightweight. I was a no-weight.

"I've got to use the restroom. I'll be back in a minute." I started for the restroom and stumbled. Sam steadied me. "I'm good!" I yelled. "I'm good!"

"Yes, you're good! You're good!" Sam yelled back, smiling. "But you're walking toward the ladies' room!"

I was hammered.

After I made it out of the restroom, Sam escorted me up the dark staircase and into the brisk air. Even though I told her I was okay, Sam insisted on walking me back to campus. Fortunately, it was all downhill. As we walked, I just started rambling about how I'd quit glee club after a year for hockey. I didn't mention that I really quit glee club for Rosemary.

"Cool," Sam smiled. "Well, ah, sing something."

"I don't know—"

"Please."

"I don't do solos."

"Look at you! I don't do solos!" Sam replied as she placed her hands on her hips. "Now I really want to hear something."

"I can't."

"A short one."

"I can't. I really can't."

"C'mon. Please!"

I didn't do solos. Never. They petrified me. But Sam wasn't backing down, and I was feeling those Special Blends. Wally's "Satan's School" was fresh, but outside of 420, it wasn't appropriate. Barry was Barry, but he didn't seem right. As we walked, I scanned the surrounding mountains. The words that I'd jotted down on the bus ride up came out.

> Took a bus up, feeling upside down.
> Just a stranger arriving in this new town.
> Trying to be strong.
> Want to prove everyone wrong.
> Figuring out what's gonna be.
> But I'm lost in the trees.
> When are you going to come back to me?

When I stopped, Sam was staring at me, her mouth agape.

"I really like your voice. . . . You must hear that a lot though."

"No, actually, I don't."

Compliments weren't the way in Castleton.

When we made it to campus, we just walked around, past the statue of the short, very overweight, retired rock star. We finally stopped in front of the steps of North South Chapel, the one that was used for storage.

"Who do you want to come back?" Sam asked as we started to walk up the steps. "I'm nosy. You don't have to tell me."

Of course, I hadn't meant to sing about Rosemary. It should've been no surprise though. I was thinking about her all the time.

"It's a long story." I shrugged and tried to hide my eyes by turning my head sideways and staring off into the night. Suddenly though, I was off balance. I'd missed a step. I held on to Sam's strong shoulder to steady myself. It was only a moment, but it felt like we had a moment—and that didn't feel right.

"I can't do this," I said abruptly, backing away.

"What? You can't wipe out on the North South Chapel steps when you're wasted?"

"I don't know," I muttered. "I just don't know."

I'm still embarrassed about what happened next. It came out quickly, a torrential downpour of emotional sewage. I told Sam about hating Castleton but desperately missing it now. I told Sam that my parents were divorced but together more than ever.

And I told Sam about Rosemary.

I told her about our three-week no-contact contract. I told her everything except that we were seeing other people. If I mentioned that, it would be more real, and I might tear up. I talked too much. Actually, I whined way too much. But Sam didn't stop listening.

When I finally shut up, Sam said, "You're cute."

"What's that mean?"

"It means you're funny. And you have nice freckles."

No one ever told me I had nice freckles.

No one, not even Rosemary.

*

After I collapsed, I immediately returned to Rosemary's family's cottage . . . but my arms were around Sam. I sat up immediately, perspiring. Where was I? Satan's School? 420? Fat Nancy's?

Sam?

What had happened?

Nothing happened, technically. But—yeah, there's that *but* again—something had happened. I'd performed a solo. I'd never done that for anyone, not even Rosemary.

Barry sing-alongs don't count!

I started planning an explanation, an alibi, but then I reminded myself that we weren't in contact. I rubbed my aching forehead. I slugged some warm bottled water from the previous day and closed my eyes. After a few moments, I was awakened by an aggressive knock.

What did my RA want now? Had he somehow found out about the fake ID?

"Hello!" said two different, familiar, frantic voices. I was trapped. Why were they here together? Weren't they divorced? I opened the door.

"My god, he's hungover!" my mother shrieked.

"Of course he's hungover, Dana!" cracked my father. "I'd be upset if he wasn't hungover. It's college. All college kids are hungover!"

"Is everything okay?" I asked nervously.

"Everything's fine. Castleton Middle School doesn't start until next week. We felt guilty about your taking the bus," my mother explained. I felt guilty about taking the bus. We were just guilty people. It's what the Mills family did. We could play full-time defendants on one of those television crime shows.

"We've come to help!"

I remained on my still bare mattress because there wasn't nearly enough space for all three of us to stand.

"Open the window!" my father blared in an agitated tone. "It smells like a distillery in here." Distillery. My father's word choice cracked me up. I stuffed my face into my mattress to conceal my laughter. Out of the corner of my eye, I saw my mom reach into her handbag. I knew what was coming, and I wanted no part of it.

"No! Please no! Please don't do it!" I ordered. "No tape measure!" My mother was a middle school teacher and an amateur interior designer. We didn't share the same taste.

"If your mother wants to tape measure, she'll tape measure!" bellowed my father, sounding a lot like Bernie Sanders. My parents were divorced, but they were a team, at least when it came to me.

"I'd prefer to do my own decorating," I grumbled.

"I love what you've done," cracked my father before turning serious. "You should listen to your mother. She has excellent taste, most of the time."

"What do you mean, 'most of the time,' Jacob?"

"Dana, you can't knock it out of the park every time. No one does."

My mother was already tape measuring away, and my father was examining my closet with a pained expression. "You don't want my help, but you need it," my mother said in her cheery, game-show-contestant voice.

"It's our help, Dana," my father interjected. "Our help!"

My mother was already locked in, and my father's agita didn't register.

"It's worse than I imagined. It's smaller than I imagined," moaned my mother.

"A cockroach couldn't live in here!" snapped my father.

"We must go to Target as soon as possible. It's an emergency!" my mother said.

"There's one about thirty-five miles away," I offered.

If they went, I'd get at least another four hours of sleep. They drove at a caterpillar's pace.

"Come with," offered my mother.

Never.

"I'd love to, but I really need to get some sleep."

"Of course he needs sleep," said my father. "He closed the saloon down last night!" Saloon.

"Dana, where's the package?"

"What package?" I asked, as I spotted the small box poking out of my mother's handbag. Maybe, just maybe, it was a reprieve from Ms. Davenport. . . .

But then I thought better of it. **Why would Ms. Davenport send me a box?**

"I can't believe I forgot," said my mother nervously.

"How could you forget that?" snapped my father.

"It was such a schlep up here. I lost my head," said my mother. "Rosemary sent you something!" When my mother said her name, our moods instantly lit up. "Her mother was supposed to drop it off before you left, but she forgot."

Forgot!? Yeah, those Luncheonette white chocolates and all that lawn mowing hadn't gotten me anywhere.

"Rosemary called, and I picked it up."

My mother reached into her handbag. Before she extended her arm, I snatched the package from her and held on to it like it was a winning lottery ticket. In her perfect penmanship, Rosemary had written my name on the front in bright red magic marker. My parents stood shoulder to shoulder in anxious silence, staring at the package, inhaling Rosemary's perfume. I felt weird about that. My parents didn't seem to care. Finally, my mother broke the silence.

"Well, aren't you going to open it?"

"Dana, let's go to Target and give Dylan some privacy," instructed my father. "If he wants to share with us later, that's up to him."

When my parents left to shop, I slowly opened the package. The note was written on Rosemary's personal stationery, which had rose vines on the edges.

> D,
>
> I hope this note still smells nice.
>
> *Yes, it does. My parents just inhaled it.*
>
> By the time you read this, I'll be off. I just want you to know how fortunate North South is to have you.
>
> *Are they?*
>
> I already miss you so much.
>
> *But I miss you more. What, are you turning this into a contest, Mills?*
>
> I'll talk to you in three weeks.
>
> *Why can't we talk now?*
>
> In the meantime, listen to this.
>
> Love you. Always.
>
> R
>
> *Wow!*

A photo of Rosemary was attached. She was on her cottage porch, smiling, her shades propped atop her head. Her hair was unusually light from the sun, and her green eyes glistened. Inside the package, there was also a Walkman cassette player with a sticky note:

> D,
>
>   Since we're not stuck in our phones, I thought it was appropriate if we go old school. Anyway, you'll probably be the only kid at North South with one of these. Enjoy!
>
>   R

A moment ago, I was exhausted. Now, I couldn't sleep. It didn't matter that Ms. Davenport had strung me along and rejected me. It didn't matter that I was at North South.

Nothing mattered.

After our three-week whatever-you-want-to-call-it, Rosemary and I would be back to us. Now, I could relax and just shut my eyes in my happy place.

When I awoke, there was an envelope underneath my door with my name on it. This one was manila and smelled like an envelope. I quickly opened it to find a note in crooked handwriting. It wasn't from Rosemary.

> Mr. Mills:
>
>   You're enrolled in my class, Sociology 101. It's an introductory class, technically, but I'm not treating it as such. I want to utilize every moment of our time. You have one and only one first year. With that in mind, please read the first three chapters of *Experiments on Mankind* before class. You also might want to look at one of my books. *Eavesdropping on America* and *Listening When No One's Listening* are two of several. They are on reserve at the library.
>
>   Also, you should know right up front I'm a dinosaur. I avoid email. I have never texted and don't plan to now or ever. However, I can be reached by phone, or even better you can drop by my office in person. We need more face-to-face, more human contact.

Last, please be on time. My definition of on time is early. I look forward to meeting you in person. Alas, my new friend, welcome to North South.

MAKE IT BETTER!

Sincerely,

Berkowitz

P.S. I have two doctorates. Many of my academic colleagues like keeping score. But please never refer to me as a doctor. I save that title for important people who do important stuff like cure cancer. I can't do that, unfortunately. Refer to me as Berkowitz, just Berkowitz. It's easier that way. Don't ask me my first name. I'll never tell. Thank you.

I wanted another envelope from Rosemary—not Berkowitz, not North South's Darth Vader. I'd already heard scant, mysterious murmurs but no specifics about "Crazy Berkowitz" and how he should be avoided at all costs.

And I wasn't ready for homework.

Is that what they even call it in college? Classes hadn't even started, and Berkowitz had given us seventy pages of reading. Seventy pages! If I were at an *it* school, I would expect that, but not here! I decided right then and there that I was going to pass on Berkowitz. I wasn't leaving North South, but I was definitely leaving Berkowitz.

As I plotted my escape, someone banged on my door. My parents couldn't be back this soon, unless they hired an Uber. They definitely wouldn't knock. It was Sam. Should I have texted her? Was that the proper etiquette? I felt guilty, but I had a rock-solid alibi: I didn't have her number.

"It's campus security. Open up!"

What now?

"Duuude, it's Wally. Open up!" Relieved, I opened the door. With his backpack slung over both shoulders and a T-shirt on, Wally looked like, well, a typical college freshman. Wally did a quick once-over of my bare mattress and walls.

"I like what you've done with the place," he cracked. "They live better in Lewisville."

They probably did.

"Where'd you disappear to last night?"

"I had a lot to drink."

"You got North Southed!"

"I got *what*?"

Wally laughed.

"It's a North South expression. When you get North Southed, you don't know which way is up or down."

"I was not North Southed."

"Maybe a little?"

"Okay, a little. I just needed some air."

"With blondie?"

"She walked me back to campus."

"There's safety in numbers," Wally grinned.

"Nothing happened," I stammered. "I told her I have a girlfriend."

Wally noticed Rosemary's large photo on my desk. How could he not? It seemed to take up a third of my closet.

"Is this the lady?" Wally asked.

"Yes, that's her."

"She's a cute one."

She was. Rosemary, however, didn't act like she knew it—because, well, she didn't. She was particularly self-conscious about her broad "linebacker shoulders."

"Are you texting each other every minute?" Wally asked.

"Well, no. We're taking three weeks off."

"Qué pasa?"

Why did I mention it? Now, I would have to explain. I felt nauseous.

"We have a no-contact contract for three weeks. We're immersing ourselves in our new lives. We want to be living and not living in our phones. We'll be stronger for it." I had myself convinced, almost.

"It makes sense," Wally replied unconvincingly.

Who cares about sense? I hated it. Wally spotted Berkowitz's note. He was in the class too, and he'd received a similar one. Unlike myself, he wasn't running for his life.

"Berkowitz. He's North South's OG," Wally said. "He volunteered to go to prison."

"What? Who on earth volunteers to go to prison?"

"Berkowitz," replied Wally. "We're in for an interesting semester."

*

"We'd love to see Fat Nancy's!" When my mother gleefully said this, I almost choked on my turkey cheddar. On their way back from shopping, my parents got lost and bumped into a local apple farm, which sold great sandwiches with homemade sour dough bread and cider. We were picnicking underneath a sweeping willow tree, which was about thirty-five yards from the basketball court where I'd fallen on my face. Another basketball game was in progress, and Sam was playing. I'd strategically positioned us so we could see the game, but the game couldn't see us. I wasn't ready for Sam to meet my parents. It would be too much, way too soon.

"Don't be ridiculous, Dana. Fat Nancy's is for young people," my father barked.

I wouldn't mention that older people went to Fat Nancy's too. After a few minutes, my mother couldn't control herself any longer.

"May I ask a question?" my mother asked.

"You may ask," I replied innocently, as I braced myself for what was coming.

"What did Rosemary have to say?"

"Dana!" my father scolded. "If Dylan wants to share, he'll share."

"She sent a photo," I said slowly.

"Just a photo?" my mother pushed.

Suddenly, I was in an interrogation room.

"She wrote a nice note too."

"Was it a note or a letter?" my father asked.

"Please, Jacob. Does it really matter?"

"I'd prefer a letter. It's more substantial. It means something. Have you replied?"

"I'll reply after our three-week sabbatical."

Finally, I had a word for it.

"Sabbatical. That's such a mature way of putting it. I miss Rosemary," my mother said wistfully.

"It's been only a few days!" I whined.

I was irritated. My parents were making me miss Rosemary more than I already did, which seemed impossible to do.

As much as I tried to ignore the pickup basketball game, I couldn't. Once again, Sam was the only female on the court. Once again, she was making guys look stupid, fortunately not me. At one point, Sam seemed to look in our direction, and I leaned behind the tree so she wouldn't spot me. As we enjoyed our sandwiches, I had a revelation: I was spying on Sam, and I was behaving a lot like my parents. I guess I was doing exactly what Rosemary wanted. I was growing.

After lunch, we returned to my closet. My mother emptied her shopping bags of purchases on my bed and ordered us out. We didn't put up a fight and went to the library to take a stab at Berkowitz's reading. I was too embarrassed to contact Mr. Wells and bail. I'd already missed the final, final deadline. I would just deal. Ms. Davenport wasn't calling. I was going to make North South work. As I read away in a cubicle, my father browsed the library's offerings. He was probably searching for something about weather, anything about weather. For my entire existence, it seemed that he'd been working on a book about the history of weather. ESPN was never on in the Mills home. It was The Weather Channel 24/7. Weather was unpredictable. Weather was excitement. We always knew when it would be partly cloudy or partly sunny anywhere in the world. Wally was born guilty. I was born into weather.

Berkowitz's reading was better than expected, but it took almost two and a half hours. If I hadn't been distracted, it would've gone down quicker. I kept thinking about Rosemary and her package. What was on the Walkman?

My phone dinged. Text.

Rosemary. She was checking in to see if I'd framed her photo and listened to the Walkman. Why hadn't I listened to it yet? I just got it.

It wasn't Rosemary.

It was my parents. My mother was done, and they were off to check out an antiques shop before it closed. I'll never understand my parents' fascination with overpriced, ancient, often broken furniture. When they were done shopping, they were headed to the motel, which was just outside North South. I assumed they were getting separate rooms, but I couldn't be certain. I'd rather eat pot gummy bears than ask if they were sharing a room to save a few bucks.

When I returned to my closet, it was unrecognizable. My mother had gone above and way beyond. My bed was made, finally. It had a new comforter, sheets, and pillows, and there was a cushion for my chair. She even placed drapes on my window. My mother did a wonderful job, but just about the entire room was in light purple. Lavender is the color. I really wished she'd gone with something darker, like navy blue, but it was done. On my wall, my mother had hung a flower collage, and she'd placed a plant on my desk. She'd also taken the liberty of framing Rosemary's photo and placing it on my desk with my Walkman. She'd gone through my desk drawer, where I'd tried to hide it. I should've known to not stash it there, but there was no room to hide anything in this place. Back in Castleton, I had space but little privacy. If I requested or even demanded it, my father would snap, "We're your parents. We should know everything!"

It was a done deal. I'd be living in an oversized, very comfortable dollhouse, but I was in a happy place. Rosemary had reached out. I left a voice mail for my parents and thanked them profusely. I got underneath my lavender comforter and laid my head on my new, fluffy pillow, and I did my favorite new activities: staring at Rosemary on my desk and listening to my Walkman. Surprise, surprise, it was Barry!

*

Lateness wasn't an option. At the very least, I could be on time. When I received Dorian's wake-up text, just in case my phone's ringer didn't go off, I was already showered and dressed.

Have fun with wild man Berkowitz. Good luck!

Dorian was an early riser too. When I was training for hockey, we sometimes ran before school. Yes, I trained hard to be a fifth-string goalie. Castleton hockey was serious stuff. All of Castleton's good players go to *it* schools. They might not quite have the grades, but they can handle a puck.

I got some coffee and some fruit and reread Berkowitz's homework. It went down easier with caffeine.

When I nervously walked into class fifteen minutes early, Berkowitz was already sitting at the front of the class behind a desk with a tall pile of papers. Berkowitz had a full head of unruly white hair and wore thin glasses on the bridge of his nose, which disguised that he was mildly cross-eyed. He wore khakis and a flannel shirt; North South professor casual. There were already eleven students in the room. I looked twice to confirm: That *was* Quarters sitting in the back with a notepad. We nodded to one another. Jackie from the freshman hike was staring down at the floor. Maybe today was a Jack day.

Wally was conspicuously absent. Perhaps he'd escaped Berkowitz after all. Smart man. As Berkowitz looked over his pile of papers, we sat in anxious silence. I studied the clock on the wall. Before we'd entered the classroom, a teaching assistant had ordered us to turn off our phones and put them away for the duration of class.

Exactly at the stroke of 8:00, Berkowitz stared at us intensely for a long moment before speaking.

"We're missing one student. . . . His loss," Berkowitz deadpanned.

"Well, who did the reading assignment?" Almost everyone raised their hand. "For those who did it, thank you. For those who didn't, thank you for your honesty. For those who are fibbing, don't be ashamed. It's human nature."

After a long moment, Berkowitz stood up and paused, examining us with his daunting, cross-eyed stare.

"Who are you?" Berkowitz asked repeatedly, as he gave each of us the once over. Did he want us to answer? No one dared. We were petrified.

"And who am I?" Berkowitz asked, before pausing. "Well . . . we have the entire semester to find out.

"Sociology 101. I know what you're probably thinking: What's this nonsense? Is this going to help me get hired for a job? The short answer is hell no! But . . . it's why we're here. It's why we're at North South. We're socialized to be here. We're supposed to go to college, right?" Wally abruptly entered the classroom, perspiring. He'd obviously been running.

"Sorry, I'm late."

"Don't say sorry," Berkowitz snapped. "Make it better! We can always make things better."

Wally took a seat in the front row. He was a brave man. Berkowitz handed out blank sheets of paper to each of us without explanation as he lectured. I took notes, but I couldn't catch everything. Here are some of the highlights:

> Well, sociology is everything. It's the brand of coffee we drink. It's the sports team we root for. It's the television show we're addicted to. When you're a sociologist, you're a reporter, an eavesdropper, a spy. Why do we do what we do? Why? Why do we think what we think? Do we think about what we do, or do we just do? Think about it. I'm proposing a revolutionary concept to you today, ladies, gentlemen, and everyone in between: I want you to think. No one's thinking. And here's another revolutionary concept: I want you to listen because no one's listening either.

> I'm your teacher. You're supposed to learn from me, right? Well, I want to learn from you. I'm a broken-down dinosaur. Everyone's communicating these days. Supposedly. But no one's connecting. No one's thinking. No one's listening. I don't get it. Please help!

> Your assignment is to give me an assignment. Give *me* something to read. There's too much darkness, so I want something positive. I want to see the light! I want you to think about something happy. What was the happiest day of your life? Don't Tweet it. Don't TikTok it. I want a document.

"Is that too much to ask?" Berkowitz asked, almost pleadingly.

Berkowitz told us he was available for us 24/7. As for the blank sheets of paper that he'd handed out at the beginning of class, it was our syllabus—kind of. There was no official syllabus. Berkowitz didn't want us to be limited.

Limited.

Rosemary didn't want to be limited either. Did her *it* school have a madman professor like Berkowitz?

"We'll figure it out as we go along," Berkowitz promised.

After seventy-five minutes, Berkowitz dismissed us.

"Make it better!" he shouted as we exited the classroom.

Immediately, I tracked down Quarters in the hallway.

"You're in this class?" I asked.

"Not officially," Quarters explained. "Berkowitz lets me sit in sometimes. Berkowitz! He's just awesome. He's better than Burning Man. A lot better."

My parents were nervously pacing outside, waiting for me to take them to my geology class, which I was agonizing over. Well, at least it wasn't organic chemistry. As best I could tell, I was the only student with parental chaperones.

The geology lecture room, which was large enough for at least four hundred students, was less than a quarter full. Wally took a seat next to me.

"Berkowitz!" Wally said enthusiastically. "I thought he was going to throw me out."

"I did too. How could you oversleep on the first day?"

"I didn't oversleep. Right before class, my mother called. I had to take it. It's tough for her to call from the inside." Out of the corner of my eye, I saw my parents listening in, attempting to figure out what Wally was talking about. Someone like Wally didn't exist in Castleton.

"Is everything okay?" I asked.

"Everything's cool," Wally said. "She's great inside. It's outside where she gets into trouble."

After class, I formally introduced Wally to my parents, and he treated them like parents. When we went to the cafeteria, they treated him like an interrogation subject, asking him every imaginable question. Wally didn't seem to mind though. In fact, he practically told them his life story, about both his parents being in prison and about growing up in foster homes.

"I've lived with forty-nine different people, give or take, in my short lifetime," Wally explained. As difficult as his life had been, he never seemed to lose his smile.

"How do you stay so upbeat?"

"Well," Wally replied, pausing. "I'm alive."

With that, my parents were silenced. They seemed embarrassed. I was. We took so much for granted.

"When are you taking off?" Wally asked my parents, breaking the silence.

"We're never leaving," laughed my father as I tried not to cringe.

"Cool," replied Wally.

No, this wasn't cool.

"Tomorrow afternoon," my mother said.

"Dana, you mean the day after tomorrow?"

"We'll play it by ear. Is that okay, Jacob?"

After Wally excused himself, we went outside where there were tables set up and *it*-school-worthy views.

"Weren't you going to introduce me?" I turned around. Sam.

"Hello, Mr. and Mrs. Mills. I'm Samantha." Samantha.

Even though she was officially no longer a Mrs., my mother didn't correct her.

When they were married, I wanted them to act married. When they were divorced, I wanted them to act divorced.

"How'd you know who we are?" asked my mother.

"We might've been professors or something," my father added. My father had always aspired to be higher on the academic totem pole than a middle school teacher. My mother didn't.

"Or something?" my mother said with a laugh.

"It's the freckles!" Sam said, smiling.

No, I wasn't planning on introducing Sam to my parents. My parents would interrogate her, and they'd interrogate me about her. My mother asked Sam to take a seat, and she proceeded to tell my parents everything she should've told me that North Southed night at the chapel.

Sam talked about growing up with a single father. Sam talked about how her mother lived far away and how she didn't see her nearly enough. Sam talked about how her father had passed on his passion of basketball to her. Sam talked about how North South was a bargain and offered her the opportunity to start immediately on the women's basketball team. Oddly, North South didn't have a men's basketball team. Sam told my parents that I'd said wonderful things about them, which I didn't recall saying. My parents could've continued to question Sam all day, and I think she might've enjoyed it. And, surprisingly, I might've too. I liked Sam. A lot. But I couldn't like Sam because Rosemary and I would be back to us, soon. It was just a matter of time, hopefully seconds. I checked my watch. Fortunately, Theater 101 was in twenty minutes. I stood up, but my parents stayed put, more than content to interrogate the day away. They were middle school teachers, but they should've been investigators.

"We got a class," I announced. "Samantha will under-stand." Sam rolled her eyes at me. She enjoyed my parents and making me squirm.

"I have a workout anyway," Sam said. "I'm actually late."

We walked out of the cafeteria together and shared an extended, formal goodbye, including hugs, before realizing that we were all headed in the same direction. Sam wound up dropping us off at class. Immediately after we took a seat in North South's theater, my parents returned to interrogation mode.

"Samantha has such beautiful hair," said my mother.

"It's so bright," said my father. "Like a comet."

"Jacob, women don't like their hair to be compared to comets."

"What do you have against comets, Dana?"

Wonderful. My parents were bickering about Sam's hair.

"Class is starting, please!" I hissed. As middle school teachers, my parents should've known better, but my parents couldn't stop.

"Did you tell Samantha about Rosemary?" asked my mother.

"Who's Samantha?" I replied.

"What do you mean 'who's Samantha'? Are you still inebriated?" scolded my father.

I forgot that Samantha was Sam.

"Yes," I whispered. "Of course, I told Samantha about Rosemary."

"What did she say?" my mother asked, not monitoring her voice.

A teacher, a flamboyant, angular woman dressed completely in white except for a long, red scarf that went down to her knees, stood in front of the class, waiting, her hands on her hips. Professor Lillian Hammerschmidt, known simply as Hammer to North South students, had a reputation for wearing bright, never-ending scarves; being no nonsense; and giving frequent, annoying pop quizzes.

"I think Samantha likes you," my mother said.

"Samantha doesn't like me!" I blurted in a louder voice than I intended, attempting to cover my hand with my mouth. "And I don't like her! I mean I like her, but I don't like her, like her!"

"What's *your* name?" Hammer asked. Hammer was from the Midwest, but she inexplicably spoke with a heavy English accent. At first, I thought Hammer was talking to me but then her eyes shifted to my mother.

"Me?" my mother asked, pointing at herself.

"Yes."

"I'm Dana Mills. I'm Dylan Mills's mother."

"And I'm his father, Jacob Mills."

I stared directly at my blank notebook, hoping to disappear.

"Is this the entire family?" asked Hammer. "Are there any siblings who were unable to make it? Cousins? Aunts? Uncles?"

"It's just the three of us," replied my mother.

"They're divorced," I interjected.

I shouldn't have, but I was retaliating for my mother creating drama in theater class.

"Interesting. And you're all here? One big happy family—that's divorced," said Hammer, nodding. "This is theater and *you are* theater!"

I didn't want to be theater. I wanted my three-week sabbatical to be over.

"It was a very pleasant divorce," explained my father.

"It was the best divorce I've ever had," my mother added, as I grimaced. Please, no more!

Unexpectedly, the class roared with laughter. Just as it was subsiding, I instinctively opened my mouth.

"It's the only divorce they've ever had!" I blurted, which provoked even more hysteria. Yeah, I was part of the problem.

After Hammer dismissed us, students ran up and introduced themselves to my parents, who basked in the attention. After all the selfies had been taken, I persuaded my parents to take me uptown. I needed a break, off campus. My parents asked me to invite Samantha and Wally, but I lied and said they were busy with other commitments. There'd been enough interrogations—for an entire semester.

After the long day, my parents returned to their motel, which was on the outskirts of North South. Back in my closet, I refused to listen to my Walkman, and I tried to avoid eye contact with Rosemary's photo. Instead, I reopened my geology textbook. I was engaged in a battle: I was determined to not procrastinate. I lasted maybe twenty-five minutes before my phone saved me from, well, rocks. It was a text. Sam. She'd sent a selfie of herself and my parents. It made me happy, which made me unhappy. I wasn't supposed to be happy, right? I wasn't sure how to respond, so I replied with a smiley face emoji. I hate emojis. It's the way to send something and say next to nothing.

I woke up early and went for a run. I didn't have to meet my parents until 8:00. We were doing breakfast and then history class. My parents were having an absolute blast at North South, and I was prepared for them to extend their trip. Fortunately, they'd missed Berkowitz's class because they had appointment at an antiques shop with odd hours. If they'd been able to attend, I have a strong feeling that the lecture would have been, well, my parents. They dropped by his office anyway.

"He has office hours. That's what office hours are for!" explained my father. "We're your parents!"

We're your parents! We're your parents! We're your parents!

Dad was always reminding me of this in an agitated tone, as if I was demanding they take a paternity test.

My parents purchased all of Berkowitz's books. Over the past few days, my parents were as happy as they'd ever been. It was nice.

But when my parents rolled into the North Pole's parking lot in their economy car, they were agitated. My mother explained that a potentially fierce hurricane might be hitting the coast, and they wanted to get an early start and "not take any chances." They were leaving immediately, hoping to make the trip in a single day. My parents were in such a hurry they didn't even bother to get out of their car. It was for the best. I didn't want to break down in the parking lot and beg my parents to take me with them to Castleton. Yeah, as much as I was trying to make North South work, I'd considered it.

Instead, I thanked my parents for visiting, redecorating, and everything else. I told them to drive safely, which was unnecessary. After they'd driven off, I stood alone in the parking lot staring at the calendar on my phone. Thanksgiving was eleven long weeks away. In two weeks though, my three-week no-contact contract, sabbatical, whatever-you-want-to-call-it with Rosemary would be history.

*

It was second semester, junior year. Hockey had just ended. We did well but not well enough, losing in the state semifinals. Castleton High, my school, has an excellent hockey program, way too good for me. I was on the team, barely. I never played, not a single second.

But I wasn't playing hockey for ice time. It was all for Rosemary, the team's manager, specifically to spend as much time with her as possible. But junior year was tough, really tough. Before preseason, Rosemary started dating Riley Kody, one of the team's best players. I couldn't blame Rosemary. Kody was The Man. He was ruggedly handsome and a genuine, decent guy as far as I could tell. I didn't deal with him much.

For most of the season, I wanted to quit the team. I hated seeing them together. I kept telling myself I was going to quit, but I never got around to it. I never get around to a lot of things. And here's the thing:

Even though she was with Kody, I still enjoyed Rosemary's company. I enjoyed our talks about whatever. Whatever is whatever probably doesn't mean a lot in the grand scheme of things.

When you're a kid, you do a lot of talking about whatever. Of course, you don't know it's whatever because you're a kid. Anyway, sometimes, Rosemary's parents didn't get along. When they'd fight, Rosemary would call me, and I'd forget that she was with Kody. Why wasn't she calling him? Afterwards, I'd see them together, and it would bring me down, again. I'd stay in my room and lie in my bed with the lights off. If I didn't have a job bussing tables at Luncheonette, the most popular restaurant in my village—not town—I just would've stayed there. The job was a lifesaver. It forced me out of my room, and the pay was nice.

Anyway, at the end of junior season, the team hosted a celebratory dance, which doubled as a fundraiser for the team's summer trip to Sweden. We didn't need a fundraiser, because everyone in Castleton—well, besides my family—is loaded, but a fundraiser sounded politically correct. I worked at Luncheonette during the summer, and I wasn't going to Sweden. No, I didn't go to the dance. I couldn't bear to see Rosemary with Kody, again. And I had work anyway. I wanted to work.

Whenever there was something I didn't want to do, I always had an out: working at Luncheonette. Luncheonette was open every day except for Christmas, and there were always shifts available. People always wanted to eat good food, and Luncheonette had the best. So I worked the night of the hockey dance; I finished up at about 11:00. As usual, I was exhausted. When I was at Luncheonette, I hustled. I focused on the task at hand and forgot what needed forgetting: Rosemary and Kody. Just as I walked out of Luncheonette, I checked my messages. "Please call me!" Rosemary pleaded, clearly upset. Immediately, I called.

"Can you meet me at the gazebo?" Rosemary asked.

"How was the dance?"

"It was a dance. People danced!" Rosemary snapped. "Will you meet me? Please!"

When I arrived, Rosemary was already there. I'll never forget the sight of her. She was still in her strapless black gown, stunning. I was speechless.

"What's wrong?" Rosemary asked.

"Nothing."

"What's wrong?" she repeated. "Please tell me."

I couldn't. I couldn't tell Rosemary that she was the most beautiful girl in the world and that I hated seeing her with Kody.

Rosemary's eyes started to well up.

"What's wrong?" I asked.

"I got home from the dance, and my parents were at it again. I just wish they'd be happy like everyone else in this town."

"Everyone's not so happy. They're just good fakers."

"Well, I wish my parents would fake it."

"Yeah, I understand. Well, at least they're honest about their feelings."

"They're honest that they don't like each other."

"Well . . . . it's more important that they love each other."

"You're right. I just—"

"I know. I know. You must focus on the good, and there's a lot of good."

"How'd you get so wise?"

"Not a clue. I'm clueless. And by the way, Castleton's a village, not a town." Slowly, a smile formed on Rosemary's face. She always said "town," and I corrected her. It was our thing.

"You're funny."

"Maybe I should be a clown and join the circus or something."

"I'll join too. Do you think they'll take a washed-up jock?"

When Rosemary made any mention of her hockey playing days, it always got to me. Unrealized potential: That was our connection. I never got to Mars or the Olympics. She never made it to the NHL.

"Well, if they'll take a washed-up underwater swimmer, I think—"

"I love you," Rosemary interrupted.

I wasn't floored by Rosemary's declaration. Rosemary had told me this before, but it was always in a friend-zone sort of way.

"I love you too," I replied back in my best friend-zone sort of way voice.

"No, I love you, love you," Rosemary repeated, looking directly into my eyes.

I was floored.

"You love me, love me?" I mumbled.

"Yes, I love you, love you! I love you, Dylan Mills!"

We stood in silence for I don't know how long. I'd dreamt of this happening for so long. Now that it was happening, I didn't know what to do or say.

"Are you going to say something, Dylan?" Rosemary finally asked, concerned. "Did I say something wrong?"

"No! You didn't say anything wrong. I'm just surprised," I said before pausing. "But Kody . . ."

"He's great. Everyone knows Kody's great. Kody knows he's great. But . . . he's not you. And I love you, Dylan."

"I love you too, always have. But . . . you already knew that."

Berkowitz, when the girl of your dreams professes her love for you, it's the happiest day of your life. Period.

Eventually, unfortunately, I wandered out of my happy place and back into my phone. No word from Rosemary. Sam hadn't responded to my emoji. Perhaps she was turned off by emojis too. It was for the best. Suddenly, my phone rang. It was an actual phone call, such a rarity. I figured it was spam, one of those bogus car warranty calls hitting me up even though I didn't have a license.

It wasn't. Dorian. It was a shot of adrenaline. We hadn't actually spoken much, but I was keeping tabs on her through her Instagram. As best I could tell, she'd already dated and broken up with someone. Before I could conduct a full-fledged interrogation, Dorian began her own. She wanted a Rosemary update. I read her Rosemary's note and told her about the photo and Walkman. I also told her about 420, "Satan's School," Fat Nancy's. And yeah, Sam.

"Did anything happen?" she asked immediately.

"No, not really."

"Not really?"

"Nothing happened, but . . ." Right after I said "but," I regretted it.

"But what?"

"I sang her a song."

"What song?"

"Just something I wrote."

"Just you and her?"

"Yeah."

"You sang a solo to her, just the two of you?"

"It was a short song."

"This is major, major, major!"

"It was a *very* short song. It wasn't even a song. It was more like a phrase."

"But you don't do solos, ever!"

"I know. I know. I had a lot to drink."

"But you don't really drink."

"I did that night."

"You like this girl?"

"Not like that."

"Why not 'like that'?"

"Well, Rosemary, of course."

"She's growing! And you're seeing other—"

"I'm not."

"Why not? Sam seems great."

"She is, but—"

"I know. I know. Rosemary."

"I'm sorry. I just can't flip a switch and start seeing other people. What do you want me to do?" Silence. When Dorian didn't reply, I thought I lost her.

"Dorian? Dorian?"

"Yes, I'm here."

"What do you want me to do?"

"I want . . ." And then Dorian stopped herself. "I want you to enjoy yourself up there, at the North Pole, wherever you are," Dorian said before pausing. "Is that really the name, or are you putting me on?"

"No, that's the name. There's a South Pole too."

"Now you're really putting me on."

"I'm not putting you on. Scout's honor."

"You were never a boy scout, Dylan Mills."

"I'm telling you: There's a North Pole and a South Pole up here."

"What names! They're smoking some great dope up there!"

"Apparently."

"Are you going to start smoking weed, Dylan?"

"No. Remember what happened with those gummy bears?"

Moments after we hung up, I got a text from Sam.

Your parents rock. Emojis, uh, not so much ☹

Bad news: Sam and I agreed on another thing: Emojis are lame.

*

Friday night. I'd survived two weeks at North South. Well, I was more than surviving. I'd stayed very focused and kept on top of my schoolwork, all of my schoolwork, not just the stuff I felt like doing. And I was ready to hand in my Berkowitz essay. I wanted it out of my hands so I could stop fussing. Yeah, I needed a time-out from my closet. I stopped by 420, but no one was home. I hung for a bit in the North Pole lounge, but the **Dandruff Duo** couldn't stop pawing one another. I wanted out, but where could I go?

Fat Nancy's.

I still had Jimmy's fake ID. My mother had promised to mail my passport, but I hadn't received it. Wally and Jimmy would probably be at Fat Nancy's later, so I decided to kill some time and take a little tour of the North South town. I'd driven around town with my parents, but I didn't see much at all. We'd gone to the same diner for every single meal, the same meal; their cobb salad special was solid. Once my parents find a good spot, they stick with it. Not long after I started my expedition, I noticed a bustling spot, a bar with an outside porch. I walked closer. Sam was hanging with a group of tall women. She didn't see me. At least, I don't think she did. I wanted to see her. But I didn't. Yeah, it was weird. I felt weird about the solo. I felt weird that she'd met my parents. And I felt weird that I didn't tell her about my parents' dinner invite. . . . But the bar looked fun, and I needed to burn time.

And, yeah, as much as I didn't want to admit it, I wanted to catch up with Sam.

But after waiting in line for about ten minutes and watching the bouncer vigilantly check IDs, I got frustrated and nervous that Jimmy's ID would fail me, and I'd land in some sort of trouble. I decided to move on. It was for the best. Contact with Rosemary was a week away. Contact with Sam would be nice but probably awkward. When I got to the corner, I looked both ways.

"Where are you going?" Sam had snuck up on me.

"Nowhere."

"You must be going *somewhere*."

"I don't know. I tried to get into the bar, but the line's a joke."

"A joke huh?" Sam smiled. "Don't say I never did anything for you."

Sam knew the bouncer, or maybe the bouncer knew her. We skipped the line. I met Sam's friends, about eight of them. As suspected, they were her teammates. Each told me their name but don't quiz me. They were friendly and not tipsy friendly because they were drinking water. Sam explained that the team had pledged a few days earlier to not drink until the season was over.

A cheesy popular song came on—something they'd probably never play in 420—and Sam and her teammates hustled inside where there was a makeshift dance floor. I felt weird about dancing with eight women, but I'd prefer that than dancing with eight men. Sorry if that's politically incorrect. Just as I was getting relaxed, Sam's teammates walked off to the side for a break and I was dancing alone with Sam, which I felt weird about. I suggested we get some ginger ales.

"They're cool, right?" Sam said, looking over at her teammates.

"Yeah, they're great."

I was envious of their camaraderie, and I was rethinking my retirement from competitive athletics. Maybe I should go out for vert disc after all.

"You'll come to a game?"

"Games," I replied.

"Good. I'm going to hold you to that."

Abruptly, an extra loud song dropped.

"My parents think you're really cool," I screamed.

"I liked them a lot too," Sam screamed back. "They're divorced?"

"Yeah."

"Why?"

"They were miserable."

"They seemed pretty happy to me."

"That's because they're divorced. . . . I don't get it, so don't ask me to explain."

Suddenly, I felt my pocket vibrating. I took out my phone.

"Who's that?" Sam asked suspiciously. I probably should've excused myself, but my heart was pounding through my chest.

It hadn't been three weeks.

When I picked up, Rosemary was hysterical, incomprehensible. I held my hand up to Sam to excuse myself and went to the restroom and sat in a stall. Rosemary's parents had gotten in a car accident. They'd hit a deer, or maybe it was a fallen tree—or both. Whatever it was, it was something bad. Rosemary didn't know. She knew that her parents were in the emergency room, and she was already on her way home.

"I need you," Rosemary whimpered.

"Hello!" I shouted. "Hello?"

Our connection was gone. Rosemary was gone. I called back, but I couldn't get a signal. When I finally did, it went straight to voice mail. It didn't matter. I knew what I needed to know: Rosemary needed me. And I knew what I needed to do. I checked the bus schedule on my phone. There was a bus departing from an adjacent town, about two miles away, in thirty-two minutes. It appeared to be the last one of the night, but I never trusted bus schedules. There was no time to wait for an Uber. I quickly scanned the bar for Sam and her teammates. Maybe one of them had a car or a scooter or a tricycle. They were so tall—human giraffes—they were impossible to miss. But they were not here. They probably had team curfew or something. I had exactly twenty-nine and a half minutes to make the bus. My parents had driven me through the town where the bus was departing from. It was a straight shot, but there was not a second to spare.

I ran out of the bar and directly into the bouncer and fell face down. In one motion, I managed to spring back up. Hockey drills were good for something.

"Dylan!" I heard Sam yell from somewhere, but I was already sprinting. I wasn't going to stop for anyone. Rosemary needed me. As I ran as fast as I could through the slight drizzle, I needed something.

I needed Barry.

I apologize for saying you're not cool, Barry. I apologize! I played Barry in my head. Barry had chops!

I kept singing until I reached the bus terminal, a run-down gas station, I keeled over. I would've vomited if I'd eaten anything.

But I was too late.

I was four minutes late. I'd failed, again, and I was devastated. I went inside the dingy room where the clerk sold tickets. "When's the next bus leave?" I panted. I'd run through several puddles, and I was drenched in perspiration and dirt. Maybe, the schedule was wrong. "You can't count on maybes," I heard my father bellow. The clerk, a tiny woman in a house gown who looked old enough to be my great-grandmother, explained that the last bus of the night was running behind schedule and hadn't arrived. I exhaled and purchased a ticket.

I cleaned up as best I could in the gas station's disgusting bathroom, but it was hopeless. When the bus finally arrived, I ran on and took one of the few remaining seats in the rear. I was forced to take a window seat next to an enormous, bearded man with a tattoo on his face and a duffel marked with the Lewisville prison logo. I didn't dare make eye contact much less exchange a greeting. He didn't adjust his manspreading one micro inch, so I had less than half a seat. I tried Rosemary again. Again, voice mail. I figured that her parents were fine. Everything in Castleton always turned out fine.

But what if, what if, it didn't this time?

I called Dorian. It seemed like someone answered, but I wasn't certain.

"Hello!" I said loudly.

Friday night, freshman year. Of course, there was loud music in the background.

"Dylan? Where are you?"

"I'm on a bus!"

"Again? What are you doing? Don't give up on North South. It's been only two weeks."

"I'm not giving up on North South!" I yelled.

The irony wasn't lost on me. Two weeks ago, all I wanted to do was give up on North South.

"Get off your phone!" barked a very angry man with a scary beard two aisles away. "Or I'll throw you off!"

I excused myself.

Moments later, my phone ran out of juice anyway, and I didn't have my charger. I hadn't brought anything, just the filthy clothes I had on. I tried to sleep but couldn't. I transformed myself into a cocoon, my head in my hands, my knees pinched together. I did everything in my power to not inhale the bus's stench, a miserable cocktail of humidity, body odor, and overcooked microwaved dinners. I wondered about the well-being of Rosemary's parents. When they learned that I was going to North South, our relationship seemed to sour even more. Of course, they weren't the only ones in Castleton. A lot of people treated me differently, at least it sure seemed that way.

Eventually, my mind wandered back to Sam. She seemed so happy to see me earlier in the evening. I regretted not turning around for her. If I'd stopped, I still would've made the bus. Of course, I didn't know that then. I would've texted her if I had any juice on my phone. But the most important thing was that Rosemary needed me, finally.

*

Yeah, you probably already know this: Castleton doesn't do buses. Just as the sun was coming up, I got off the bus in Castleton's adjacent town. Fortunately, the hospital wasn't too far. No one was at the hospital's front desk, so I just walked in and started checking names on rooms. Sure, I should've waited for an attendant, but I wasn't thinking after the all-night ride. It didn't matter. All of the rooms seemed empty.

"Who are you?" a woman in light green scrubs asked sharply and condescendingly.

"I'm Dylan Mills. I was born in this hospital."

"Never heard of you."

"Which room are Mr. and Mrs. Silversmith in? I'm a family friend."

"Sir, that's confidential information."

"It's urgent," I pleaded. "Are they even here?"

"Are you going to make me call security?"

I ran out and scoured the parking lot for Silversmith cars. As best I could tell, none were there. If the Silversmiths had been admitted, they'd checked out. They must be fine. Everything turned out fine in Castleton.

Or maybe they were in another hospital?

I didn't know what to do, but I wasn't going home.

Rosemary's room was on the second floor. I had lots of experience climbing to her room, often in the dark. There was always a sturdy wheelbarrow right below her window, which I propped myself up on. A great sign: The Silversmith's driveway seemed full, and there was no noticeable damage to any of the cars. Rosemary's car was there too.

But there was no wheelbarrow.

I should've just waited to go home, where my mother was living without my father, and wait.

But I didn't want to wait anymore.

It had been too long, almost fourteen days, almost 336 hours. On the third jump, I got a hold of the window's ledge and pulled myself up. I was within inches of Rosemary spotting me and opening the window, as she'd done so many times before. I could practically inhale her scent. Suddenly though, I felt an unbearable surge of pain in my calf: a cramp. I lost my grip and fell to the ground, landing awkwardly on my right ankle. Somehow, I didn't scream, but still a neighbor might've heard. If they did, it would be only a matter of seconds before Castleton's aggressive private security team were summoned by an overly cautious neighbor. Castleton had no shortage of those. If Quarters dared step into this village, I imagined, he'd be promptly surrounded and escorted to the village's lines. Anyway, I didn't need an arrest at Rosemary's on my résumé.

I must escape.

I pushed myself off the ground and stood up, mostly on my left leg and limped back to the center of town and the gazebo. As I limped along, I couldn't bear to look at my swollen ankle. I needed a break and lay down on the perfectly manicured lawn. I'd rest for just a moment. But as soon as my head hit the ground, I was gone. I probably would've slept there all day if the Castleton groundskeepers weren't meticulous, *always* keeping the grass an exact two and a half inches.

When I opened my eyes, Luncheonette's brunch line was out the door. I walked on the opposite side of the street with my head down so no one would see me in such a sorry state, and I picked up my pace as much as I could. As I turned a corner though, I nearly bumped into a tall, muscular kid wearing an oversized, black hoodie. When we made brief eye contact, I could've sworn that he glared at me. He looked familiar, particularly his piercing black eyes, but I couldn't place him. Who was this kid, and what was his problem? When I was almost home, it came to me: It was Kody, Rosemary's ex. But how could it be? Kody was off at his *it* school playing hockey and doing Kody things. I didn't obsess over Kody too long though. My ankle hurt like hell.

When I finally arrived at my front lawn, my mother was loading the car with her tennis racquet. A few months earlier, she'd started playing, lessons and everything.

"Mother Mills!" I announced, attempting joy.

"Dylan!" she gasped.

"It's just a slight sprain."

"You're bleeding!"

Somehow, in addition to everything else, I'd scraped my forehead.

Immediately, mixed doubles was canceled.

My mother whisked me inside and sat me down on the couch. She cleaned my forehead, wiped it with alcohol, and applied a bandage. I showered with my right sneaker on.

My mother took me to the hospital, the same one I'd visited earlier. It was still empty, and there was no wait. The doctor took some precautionary X-rays. Fortunately, it was a sprain, not a break. She prescribed painkillers and put me in a walking cast, fortunately all covered by my parents' health insurance. My mother stopped at a deli near the hospital and got me bagels and two large waters. North South didn't do bagels. I ate heartily because I was starved—and a mouthful of bagel would postpone the imminent interrogation.

"Why are you home?" my mother finally asked.

"It's a long story. I have a headache," I said somberly between bites. "Can I tell you later?"

"Just tell me this," asked my mother.

"What?"

"Does it involve Rosemary?"

"Everything involves Rosemary. You know that! But can we talk about it later?"

My mother wasn't satisfied, but she dropped the interrogation, at least momentarily. If it involved Rosemary, all was forgiven.

I woke up after 2:00 and felt a lot better. When I checked my messages, I had two from Dorian but nothing from Rosemary. I immediately called Rosemary, and she picked up immediately.

"Are your parents okay?" I asked before she could get a word out.

"Everything's fine, just a few bumps and bruises. They weren't even admitted to the hospital," she said matter-of-factly.

"Well, that's great."

"And insurance will cover the car. It wasn't that bad at all. I overreacted."

"No. You didn't know. It's wonderful that they're okay."

I felt foolish. Rosemary didn't need me. I was the one that was needy. I'd behaved as if the sky were falling, and everything was fine. Just like I told you: Everything always turns out fine in Castleton.

"Where are you?" Rosemary finally asked.

"I'm home."

"You came home for me?"

"Of course."

"You didn't have to," Rosemary said in her high-pitched, gentle voice, which was nice to hear. However, I couldn't quite pinpoint it, but she sounded different. Maybe it was the painkillers. Or maybe I was overanalyzing, again.

"Of course, I had to. You needed me. You told me you needed me," I wanted to say. Instead, I said, "I wanted to. I'm here for you."

"I know. You always are. Well, thank you."

"You're welcome."

Our mutual courtesy struck me as flat-out wrong. I don't recall us thanking each other before.

"I love you!" I just about yelled out with Stanley Kowalski urgency.

I was reading *A Streetcar Named Desire* for Hammer. I felt like it'd been bottled up. Now that I released it, I wanted to hear it back. I know that's wrong, but—

"I love you too," replied Rosemary. She said it in an almost obligatory tone, almost like she didn't say it.

But she did say it. SHE SAID IT!

We made plans to meet at about 9:00. Of course, I wanted it to be earlier, but Rosemary had parental obligations, understandably. In case you're wondering, Mr. and Mrs. Silversmith had hit a fallen branch, a large one. As I recovered and rested, I felt dumb. After all this, I was a lot more banged up than Rosemary's parents.

"Oh, the irony," I imagined Hammer commenting in her strange English accent.

I checked in with my father and explained why I'd returned. It was easier to discuss with each parent separately. If I explained it to them at the same time, a conversational ping-pong would ensue, and guess who'd be the ball? I explained that Rosemary had asked me to come. She hadn't explicitly, but it was ballpark. "You're a good friend," my father told me. I know he had more questions, but before he had a chance to ask, I changed the subject to something he enjoyed almost as much as Rosemary.

Weather.

"Why'd you get hooked?" I asked.

"Well," he answered slowly. "I wasn't the most outgoing kid, and weather gave me a ticket to talk to anyone. Everyone wants to know about the weather. As far as conversation, it's the great equalizer."

Our usual meeting place was the gazebo, but Rosemary was picking me up because of my ankle.

"It's a new era," Rosemary declared over the phone, which provoked a tinge of sadness. I wanted the old era. My mother dropped her plans, and my father dropped back by. Rosemary was home. It was an event.

My parents asked Rosemary every imaginable question about school. I felt awkward because my parents were talking to Rosemary before I even got a chance to. It had been only two weeks, but it felt like two years.

After about twenty-five minutes, we finally escaped. I didn't make up an excuse to get out of the there. Is that growth?

In the car, I inhaled Rosemary's scent—finally. It was slightly different from what I was used to, but it was still glorious. My hand found her smooth, warm hand, and a jolt went through me. At a red light, I leaned over, but before I could bury my face in her neck, a car honked.

Green light.

"We must be careful," Rosemary cautioned.

Yeah, I'd lost my head. Rosemary could do that.

"Your parents have the best divorce," Rosemary laughed.

"Or the worst, depending on how you look at it. They're divorced, but they're acting married."

Immediately after I said it, I imagined being married to Rosemary. Where would we live? Would we live in Castleton? Probably not. We couldn't afford it. What would we be able to afford?

"What are you thinking?" Rosemary asked in her cutesy voice, abruptly cutting off my fantasy.

"Ah nothing," I stammered. "Are you up for Nobody You Know?"

NYK, a diner just outside Castleton, was a diner with a jukebox, pinball, and sandwiches—all amazing.

"I already ate. I'm so full," said Rosemary.

And then I bit.

"What do you have in mind?"

"They're having a few kegs at the Castle," Rosemary said cheerfully.

No, absolutely not, I wanted no part of the Castle. Hadn't we already heard that song? But, yeah, Rosemary called the shots.

"It'll be fun."

"Sounds like a blast," I deadpanned.

"It will be!" Rosemary insisted with a laugh as she tapped my shoulder. "Just like old times!"

Old times? We'd been away two weeks. But I wanted old times with Rosemary, so maybe this could be good.

We parked the car at the service road entrance. I was here mere days ago, but it *was* a new world. The Castle belonged to the next group, people we barely knew, if at all. Let's be clear: I never felt that the Castle belonged to me, but now it felt like it really didn't belong to me.

Yeah, it was a new era.

As we approached the Castle, Rosemary smiled. "This is going to be so much fun," she gushed. "We're like the returning conquering heroes."

Rosemary was the hero. She was at the *it* school. I was . . . what was I? Please don't answer that.

But I played along and frowned inside. Within moments of reaching the crowd, Rosemary started embracing kids she barely knew as if they were long-lost friends. She probably didn't even know their names, but she was a good pretender. I didn't recall her being this good.

When I turned around, Rosemary had a beer in her hand. I couldn't drink because of the painkillers. Doctor's orders. I watched Rosemary interact. She had a wonderful smile; her skin was smoother than ever. It was hard to believe that Rosemary didn't think she was attractive. As Rosemary hugged away and exchanged generic pleasantries, I walked off to a table where there were some below average chips and pretzels that would be gone in minutes. I was hungry, and I might seem less needy if I had an activity.

"What happened to you, bro?" asked a kid I vaguely recognized as I bit into a potato chip.

"I just fell awkwardly."

"That sucks."

"Yeah."

Welcome to high school keg chatter. Were these the glory days of high school that everyone was nostalgic for?

Just to hold on to something, I grabbed a beer. I also filled one up for Rosemary.

"Isn't it great to be back? This is fun!" she beamed.

"Yeah, it's nice," I replied, forcing a smile.

Rosemary smiled back and rubbed my shoulder affectionately. And just as there was a glimmer of a connection, a few girls in nearly identical floral dresses grabbed Rosemary away.

"You're not going to believe this!" they squealed.

No, I can't believe this! I'm back at the Castle. Two weeks ago, I swore I'd never be back.

Was this growing?

I wanted to shrink.

Feeling neglected and annoyed is not a good look on anyone, at least that's what my father always tells me, so I tried everything in my power to fake it. But I didn't succeed. As Rosemary did her thing, I put on a fake smile and pretended that I was being asked about North South.

Does North South have a football team?

No. We have a bong team! And we're awesome. I mean if we don't win the national title, it's devastating. And it's not luck. We recruit the best stoners from everywhere!

How are the classes?

They're a trip! We're allowed to smoke dope in class, that's when we're there, which we never are!

Why's it called North South?

We're so stoned all the time, we don't know which way is up! We even have a term for it. It's called getting North Southed!

I ordered an eggplant and mozzarella on a baguette from our favorite spot, Sandwich Shop, which delivered to the Castle. By the way, just in case you're wondering, heroes and hoagies don't exist in Castleton. I offered Rosemary half, just like the old days. I assumed she'd decline.

"You're going to make me fat," Rosemary whined in a low voice. Rosemary's mention of her weight surprised me. She just wasn't that kind of girl.

"I'll have a bite, just a small one."

Rosemary wound up splitting the sandwich with me. She was on her third or fourth beer, which surprised me. She'd never been a huge drinker. I learned later that she smoked half a joint too. She must've done that while I was making friends with the potato chips.

After I ditched my full beer, I completely surrendered to my foul mood. I was tired of the Castle and pretending that these kids were my BFFs—or that I even knew who they were. I was exhausted from the miserable bus trip. And yeah, I was depressed Rosemary didn't need me. *I* was needy. My sprained ankle hurt like hell. I hated North South. I went to an *it* school—for dope, and I didn't even smoke. I was the dope! I hated Castleton. I hated the fact that Rosemary and I would never be us again. Yeah, I was pissed off.

And then, suddenly, Rosemary clasped my hand, and it was as if a bolt of electricity shot through me.

"Let's get out of here," Rosemary whispered. She reeked of alcohol and weed, but I didn't care.

"We should call an Uber. We can get your car in the morning. Plan?"

"Yeah, I wish you had a license."

"Me too."

Rosemary squeezed my hand tighter and our shoulders touched. Her scent was diminished greatly by the beer, but it was still her scent.

"It's all right. You'll get it," Rosemary reassured. "Come here."

She placed her hand around my head, pulled me to her and laid one on me. There was no such thing as a bad Rosemary kiss. However, this one was sloppy and aggressive. Drunken.

It was after midnight when the Uber dropped us off at Rosemary's house. We went through the front door and quickly tiptoed up the stairs to her room, where I inhaled the unmistakable aroma. I wanted to somehow bottle it and transport it back to my North South closet. As much as I don't want to admit it, there were moments during the past two weeks when I thought I'd never be in this room again.

"It means a lot that you're here," Rosemary whispered as we looked into one another's eyes. "I can always count on you."

Any pain in my ankle was gone.

*

When I opened my eyes, it was before dawn. Rosemary was already showered and dressed, ready to return to her *it* school. She had a long ride, and a lot of schoolwork. I was disappointed. I'd been hoping that we'd brunch at Luncheonette. I wanted to return as a civilian. With her.

"You want a ride home?" Rosemary asks. Her car is still at the Castle. She'll use one of her parents'.

"You should rest. You have a long trip. I'll Uber."

"It is a haul," Rosemary groans.

"I know. You should get an early start."

I kiss Rosemary's forehead and quietly leave.

Since Friday night, I'd been completely focused on Rosemary. It was almost as if North South hadn't happened. For a few hours, we were us. Now, just like that, we aren't.

When I return home, my mother is pretending to be busy in the kitchen. She's never up this early on a Sunday. We have coffee and pretend that everything is normal, which, of course, it isn't.

Rosemary was back, kind of.

But my mother pretends to play it cool and not bombard me with questions about her. Instead, we talk about North South. She asks about Wally and Berkowitz.

And Samantha.

I thank my mother again for taking care of my ankle and me.

She gives her standard reply.

"I'm your mother," she replies warmly. "It's what I signed up for." She says it as if it were military service.

After a quick shower, I took an Uber over to my father's studio apartment, in the next town over from Castleton, a much cheaper option. He's been there for months, but it still looks as if he'd just moved in. Besides the bare necessities and an antique lamp, which does not turn on, there's nothing. As I rode back home, I thought of him in his bare studio, alone. Divorce didn't suit him.

Luncheonette had its usual, long brunch line. As soon as I walked through the door, Mr. Nillson embraced me and asked where I wanted to sit. I couldn't, I explained. I just came by to see the family—the Luncheonette staffers. Most, if not all, of them didn't have the opportunity to attend college. North South was as good as any.

When I visited the kitchen, the brunch hustle was well underway, a whirl of flames, hot plates, and some of the finest cuisine anywhere. As busy as things were, everyone took a moment to acknowledge me with a warm smile, even an embrace if I was close enough, no conversation necessary. Chef, who was always agitated, asked if he could make me an oyster omelet, which wasn't on the menu. Chef never prepared meals that were off the menu. I had a bus to catch, so I reluctantly passed.

As I limped out of Luncheonette, I did a double take. My heart leapt.

She was here.

Rosemary had driven up to the curb. I was ecstatic but also confused.

"Hey there," Rosemary said with her confident smile. She was dressed casually in jeans and a baseball cap. Her hair was in a ponytail. She made it work. She could make anything work.

"What happened?" I asked.

"A girl has got to eat! And why not eat at the best place in town?"

"It's a village, hon."

Rosemary playfully punched my shoulder.

When Mr. Nillson spotted us, he proceeded to give us the treatment that he reserved for heads of state—and heads of state dined at Luncheonette. Mr. Nillson plucked us from the line and directed us to a prime corner table near the window. Rosemary smiled, impressed. Right then and there, I had the urge to tell her that I loved her. But the timing seemed off.

After we sat, I removed my fleece, and Rosemary winced ever so slightly. I was wearing my bright orange North South long sleeve, the one with the upward arrow in front of the N and the downward arrow in front of the S. At first, I'd found North South's colors and logo to be disconcerting, but they'd grown on me.

"What's wrong?" I asked. I shouldn't have.

"Nothing," Rosemary replied unconvincingly.

"What?" I prodded. I shouldn't have.

"I really liked that fleece that you were wearing just a moment ago," she explained.

"You don't like my North South shirt?" I wanted to ask.

Instead, I excused myself and went to the restroom and put my fleece back on. Bye-bye North South shirt. Perhaps this was a good thing. Back in our old era, Rosemary was always commenting on my outfits. Maybe the old era was bridging over to the new era. Maybe, just maybe, we were growing—together.

And then I heard my father's voice again: "You can't survive on maybes!"

When Mr. Nillson arrived with a special tasting plate, Rosemary glowed.

"They love you," Rosemary said.

"I love you," I wanted to say but didn't because I didn't want to seem needy.

"It's a special place with special people."

It was cornball chatter, but I meant it. For months, I'd dreaded Luncheonette and the snide murmurs about North South. Now, there was no place I'd rather be. I didn't eat much, but Rosemary ate heartily. She was hungover. Even as she stuffed her face, I couldn't keep my eyes off her. Rosemary was wearing an acorn necklace, something I'd never seen on her before. Rosemary explained that the acorn necklaces were produced by TTK, who was selling them from his popular Instagram account for $50 a pop.

"How didn't you hear about these things?" she asked. "Where have you been?"

"I've been at the North Pole."

"What?" Rosemary asked. How could she not know the name of my dorm? Then again, I didn't know the name of her dorm. We had so much to catch up on but not nearly enough time.

"I'm not an Instagram dude. You know that." At least she used to know.

"Dude? I've never heard you say that."

Dude just wasn't in the Castleton vocabulary. And when Rosemary said it, she did it without Wally's flair.

"It's cool. A lot of the hockey players at school call each other dude. It's always 'dude this, dude that.' It's funny." Rosemary was her school's hockey team manager, at least one of them. They had a lot.

Suddenly, the compact, judgmental man that was in my ear these past two weeks was standing over me. Mr. and Mrs. Z were making their rounds.

And just like that I hated Castleton, again. Mr. and Mrs. Z asked Rosemary a lot of rhetorical questions about her school.

"Isn't the campus spectacular?" How many times was I going to hear that? I'll get you a postcard. I masked my grimace, at least I think I did. I just had to ride this out for a few minutes, and they'd vanish.

But they didn't.

They turned their attention to me.

"Didn't Bob Dylan go to North South?" Mr. Z asked. When I heard Mr. Z utter North South, I almost spit out my water.

"No, but North South has a great music department. Some very respected musicians have attended."

"Who?"

"I can't remember."

I should've known the jam band member.

"You don't remember?" It was a question, but it sounded like an indictment. Before I could reply, Mr. Z rifled his next attack. "Do you know if they graduated?"

Do I look like the registrar? And did it even matter? Either way, they've done pretty well. But instead of saying any of that, I blankly replied, "I don't know."

Mr. Z gave me the creeps, and I just couldn't deal.

When the silence became too awkward, I changed the subject and mentioned that I was considering auditioning for North South's nationally recognized a cappella group. The Zs listened intently, maybe a little too intently, like it was work. Abruptly, I turned the conversation on its head.

"How are you?" I asked.

"Same old, same old," replied Mr. Z. Mr. Z was pleading the fifth.

Before I could blink, the ball was on my side of the net.

"Didn't those escaped prisoners pose as North South students for half a semester?" Mr. Z pestered.

Following Mr. Z's jibe, I might've winced, but I didn't flinch.

"They made Dean's List," I snapped.

"Really?" The Zs and Rosemary practically shouted in unison. "How 'bout that?"

"No, that was just a bad rumor," I smiled. "North South actually helped capture them."

I wasn't bussing tables now. I had silenced my sarcasm for too long.

When the Zs finally excused themselves to grace another table, Rosemary grabbed both my hands enthusiastically, looked into my eyes and told me what I had wanted to tell her earlier.

*

I'd lost all sense of time, and I missed the last bus back to North South, so I stayed in Castleton another night. I'd miss Monday's classes. My mother made pasta with a great sauce, and my father joined us, contributed an amazing Greek salad. I couldn't remember the last time we were all together for a home-cooked feast.

After dinner, I stared at photos on my phone from my surprise birthday party, which Rosemary had thrown for me senior year. Suddenly, I had an idea: I'd surprise Rosemary for her birthday, which was less than a month away. Right then and there, before the flights became insane, I purchased plane tickets. Done. I was surprising Rosemary for her birthday. I was exhilarated and couldn't sleep. I checked out TTK's growing social media mini empire.

"Peace, love, and everything in between," it said at the top of his Instagram, below his initials. There was no mention of his, ah, unique upbringing. Another thing: Rosemary's necklace didn't look like it was worth anywhere near $50. Yeah, TTK was just doing it the Castleton way: overcharging. After everything he'd endured, I was genuinely happy for TTK. I purchased two acorn necklaces.

On the bus ride back to North South, I started Berkowitz's *Eavesdropping on America*. Berkowitz had rented an RV and traveled across the country one summer. He didn't speak to a soul, but he reported what he heard and observed. Maybe Rosemary and I could travel across the country after graduation. An RV wasn't her style. Yeah, I was getting ahead of myself, again. Wouldn't be the first time.

It had been only a few weeks, but Rosemary was different. She looked different, smelled different. She was as beautiful as ever, even though she was inebriated or hungover for almost all of our very brief time together. She'd gained a few pounds, nothing crazy but noticeable. With all the uphill walking to town, it was tough to put on weight at North South. Perhaps North South should put that in their pamphlet.

Or maybe it was me.

After a few weeks at North South, I felt different. And Castleton seemed way different. I felt almost like an alien in this village. Who were these perfectly manicured, pompous people? And my parents, they were different too. They weren't just parents. They were human beings too. It was two weeks, but I felt much older. Maybe, I was growing.

As soon as I got back to campus, I texted my parents. I was psyched to lay down in my cozy closet. But when I entered, it was empty. My bed was gone. As I sat on the floor of my closet, I contemplated this: Who would take my bed, my lavender bed? Fortunately, everything else was intact. I was surprisingly calm about all this, or maybe it wasn't surprising at all. Rosemary and I were good, which meant everything was good. Everything else would work out. I was in a happy place. I had myself to blame for the bed. I didn't lock my door. We never locked our doors in Castleton. In our private security enclave, we felt untouchable, above it all. I'm not proud. As I walked over to my RA to investigate the case of my missing lavender bed, Wally appeared.

"Duuude, what happened to you?" he asked, eyeing my walking cast.

"I had a little accident. No big deal."

"You went MIA?"

"I had to go home."

"Is everything—"

"Everything's good. Everything's great. But someone stole my bed."

"I just saw a bed out on the basketball court with purple sheets."

Fortunately, the players had moved my bed off the court so they could play. Fortunately, it hadn't rained, and fortunately Sam wasn't around to witness. She'd already seen me in enough embarrassing positions.

"Who would do such a thing?" I asked Wally.

"I know exactly who would do such a thing," Wally replied without hesitation. "Sherbert!"

"What's a Sherbert?" I asked.

Wally laughed.

Sherbert was a skinny stoner with a heavy lisp and a bizarre man bun that sometimes pointed straight up like the Eiffel Tower. He supposedly once ate four gallons of orange sherbert, which earned him his nickname. Sherbert enjoyed getting stoned and playing pranks, mostly stupid, harmless stuff. He'd already wrapped up at least a dozen passed-out freshman in toilet paper and drew horrendous cartoons on their faces.

"I'm going to teach Sherbert a lesson," Wally declared, as he started for the door.

"What are you going to do?" I asked, stepping in front of him.

"Payback!"

Wally was a very strong man. I'd never met Sherbert, but my guess was that this lispin' stoner wasn't.

"You shouldn't."

"Why not? You gotta stick up for yourself."

"Yeah, but I have a better idea."

"What?"

"Reparations."

"Reparations," repeated Wally. "I like the sound of that."

"Good."

"Just one thing."

"What?"

"What are reparations?"

Before he ran out, Wally asked if he could check out my Berkowitz essay. He needed inspiration. It was personal, but I was showing it to Berkowitz, so why not Wally.

A little later, Wally was back with an enormous grin.

"I got a surprise for you," Wally declared, delicately waving a small plastic bag. "Reparations! Sherbert gave it as a peace offering. His stuff is super potent."

"Great but I don't smoke."

"Can you at least keep a brother company?"

Because of my ankle, we took our time walking over to the lake. When we found a chill spot, Wally took out his pipe, which he'd decorated with a North South decal, and he inserted Sherbert's weed. He lit up, slowly inhaling before exhaling. After the miniature clouds had disappeared into the dusk, Wally smiled and handed me the pipe.

"I'm good," I said.

"Cool. Your Berkowitz thing was nice."

"Thank you."

"Rosemary! She's awesome."

"She is. She's kind and smart and funny. And she's a beautiful girl, inside and out. And she's just the best with my parents."

"She's your high."

"I never thought of it that way but yeah."

Wally had nailed it.

As we listened to the crickets, I felt calm in a weird sort of way, and Wally just started talking.

"You never wanted to get too close with anyone at the foster homes. It was a revolving door; people always coming and going. And everyone wanted to forget that they were there in the first place."

Wally's words hung in the late summer air, and I didn't utter a syllable. What could I say? Nothing seemed to change in Castleton, and when things seemed like they might go bad, everything always seemed to turn out fine. And of course, there were no foster homes in Castleton. TTK was the closest thing we had to a foster child, but he was more adjusted than most of the natives. Somehow, he'd become an expert snowboarder almost immediately. A few of my classmates dubbed him Osama Ski Laden.

I was out of it. I was stoned; at least I think I was stoned. Wally's secondhand smoke was more than enough to do the trick. Fortunately, I wasn't nauseous, but I was in no shape to do anything.

When Wally was done, it was pitch black, and I was sleepy and disoriented. Wally walked confidently down a walking path, and I followed. But when we exited the woods, we were on the wrong campus, at the college across the lake. Rich & Dumb's identical limestone buildings were perfectly placed on a series of perfect rolling hills, all interconnected by perfectly paved limestone paths, which were dotted by matching black streetlights. Rich & Dumb was Instagram ready. Just so you know, Rich & Dumb isn't the school's actual name. It's what North South students called it. Ridge & Day was a wannabe *it* school, whose student body had a reputation for being spoiled, entitled stoners.

R&D had laundry service.

North South and R&D despised one another. On our campus, they were "Rich Dummies." On their campus, we were "North Stoners." We considered R&D to be our rivals, but they refused to acknowledge us. The Dummies refused to play us in athletics, including vert disc. R&D claimed to be vert disc's birthplace. According to Quarters, when he started it, he invited anyone and everyone to participate, including Rich Dummies, who learned the game at North South before starting their own squad.

Almost immediately, an R&D security guard identified Wally and me as intruders. It wasn't difficult. Our bright orange North South sweatshirts were a dead giveaway. He checked our North South IDs and let us off with a warning. Wally called someone to pick us up. As we were leaving, I overheard a security guard say, "Those North Stoners were stoned out of their freakin' gourd!"

When I finally made it back to my closet, a terse email from my history professor, Mr. Victor, sobered me up a little. I was surprised. I thought that skipping class was permitted in college. I didn't expect North South to be such sticklers. When Rosemary and Dorian missed class, they didn't hear boo. I emailed back an explanation without getting too specific and promptly fell asleep, only to be awoken shortly after by my phone. It was a text.

Rosemary.

> I hope you had a safe, fun bus trip back. Thanks again for looking out.

As ecstatic as I was to hear from her, I would've preferred an actual call. Texting was my least favorite form of communication. Berkowitz described texting as "pizza without the crust." In my stoned state, I couldn't stop reading those two sentences. Why are you hoping that I had a safe trip back? Doesn't that go without saying? And why are you hoping it was fun? Buses are practical and reasonably priced but not fun. And why are you thanking me? We never thanked each other before.

I was overanalyzing, again. And I was stoned. I think. I texted Rosemary back, told her about Wally and getting lost, but I didn't mention my missing bed episode or Sherbert's potent weed. I didn't want to diminish North South's fragile reputation any more than it already was in her mind. But after I hit send, I decided to address something that was gnawing at me. I typed it out.

> Why do you have a problem with my North South long sleeve?

Should I hit send? Should I say something else? ANYTHING? What should I say? Before I did anything, I passed out.

*

We were underwater. Swimming. I was in the Castleton pool, desperately trying to catch up to Rosemary. My parents were standing, encouraging me to go faster, and I did. But as hard as I tried, I couldn't catch Rosemary.

When I finally came up for air, I was soaked in perspiration. I was in my closet; the morning sun was strong. I'd slept for ten hours, but I felt like I hadn't. There was another text.

> Have a great day! Wally sounds like an interesting dude ☺

I was happy, but I wasn't happy about the emoji. If you have something to say, say it! And I started thinking about all those hockey dudes at Rosemary's *it* school. I didn't like that they were around Rosemary all the time—and that I wasn't.

Panic! It was 8:02. I was late for Berkowitz. I never slept late. I also never smoked weed. I hadn't, but I had. I sprinted to class in my pajamas, my bright orange North South sweats. I looked like a wrinkled tangerine. Fortunately, class was only about two hundred yards away. When I ran into class, I was perspiring and breathing hard.

"Thank you for joining us, Mr. Mills," said Berkowitz with his usual sarcasm.

"I'm sorry," I replied, quickly scanning the room.

Wally wasn't here again.

"Don't be sorry. Make it better!" ordered Berkowitz. "Do you have my reading?"

"Yes, I have it," I replied, reaching into my folder.

No, it wasn't there. I'd given my hard copy to Wally. "No, I'm very—I don't. I'll have it for you later today."

"No rush. It's just sociology."

A moment later, Wally appeared.

"Another dramatic entrance from Mick Jagger!" declared Berkowitz. "Thank you for joining us." Berkowitz had started referring to Wally as Mick Jagger. There was a resemblance. Both had longish black hair, but Wally was bulkier, had much thinner lips, and, yeah, was half a century younger.

"Do you have my reading, Mr. Jagger?"

"I'm working on it. You'll have it soon."

"Soon is vague but more optimistic than later."

"Also, sir, I have Dylan Mills's assignment, but I misplaced it."

"Why are you calling me *sir*? And why did you have Mr. Mills's assignment?"

"Ah, well . . . I needed inspiration."

"Inspiration is vital. Where do you think Mr. Mills's assignment is?"

"Ah, I don't know."

"You don't know?"

"It's a long story."

"We have time. Please share. I love a good yarn."

"You really want to know?"

"If I didn't want to know, I wouldn't ask."

"I got a care package."

"Care packages are wonderful, especially when they involve sweets."

"Well, ah, it was weed, and it was more potent than I expected. It really inspired me to write something, but then I fell asleep, and I overslept. When I woke up, I looked everywhere for Mr. Mills's paper, but it was gone. I apologize."

"Do not apologize. Make it better!"

"Okay, well, I'll take back my apology."

Everyone, including Berkowitz, laughed.

"Excellent! If I were grading today's class, Mr. Jagger, what grade do you think you would receive?"

"You'd flunk me."

"Absolutely not. I'd give you the highest possible grade. Do you know why?"

"No," Wally replied. "I really don't."

A few students laughed nervously.

"You didn't succeed today, but you were completely honest about it, which is refreshing."

"Thank you," Wally said cautiously. "I think."

"Do you know why it's refreshing?"

"I don't think so."

"EVERYONE LIES THEIR ASSES OFF!"

Berkowitz proceeded to lecture us on how our society was completely inundated with lies. We lied as much as we blinked. We lied to our friends, to strangers, to machines. We lied so much that we didn't even know we were lying. Berkowitz ordered us to consume ourselves with lies: Lies told. Lies received. Lies overheard. Kid lies. High school lies. College lies. Adult lies. Every lie imaginable. I was invigorated by Berkowitz, but I was also troubled.

I'd told a lot of lies.

Wally felt genuinely bad about the paper. He could've sworn he placed it on his desk, but after Sherbert's batch, he wasn't sure. It was no big deal. I'd print out another copy and drop it off at Berkowitz's office. I had other things on my mind.

Rosemary.

I wanted to define our relationship. Were we back to us or . . . ? I knew that we could never be the Castleton version of us. She was at her *it* school, and I was at the North Pole, but maybe we could be us *2.0*. I was determined to have an actual live conversation, not a text with a stupid emoji. I wanted a pizza with the crust, all the toppings. But I also felt like I was walking a tightrope. If I pushed too hard—if I seemed needy—I risked pushing her away.

I called Dorian, to hear me out. I really needed her to listen, but I wound up listening to her about her troubles with her latest boyfriend, who was "hard to read." I laughed to myself. I was an open book. Before I could get to Rosemary, Dorian had to run to class. After we hung up, I called Rosemary.

Straight to voice mail.

As I sat in the cafeteria, I took out my notebook and started thinking of lies for Berkowitz.

> I'll just have one bite.
> This is the truth.
> I'm not lying.
> I'll call back.
> Did you lose weight?
> I lost weight.
> This is the last time.
> This is the first time.
> It'll take one minute.
> I love you.

I love you.

When Rosemary said it at Luncheonette, it didn't sound like a lie. But when she said it in her car earlier, it didn't sound like the truth.

Did Rosemary love me—or was it all a lie?

When I dropped my paper in Berkowitz's box outside his office, his door was halfway open.

"Who's that?" Berkowitz growled as if I were trespassing.

"It's Dylan Mills," I replied, managing to stay out of his sight. "I'm in your Sociology 101 class."

"What are you playing hide-and-seek for? Get in here!" Berkowitz ordered. "And bring whatever you put in my box. I removed my paper and entered his office. I wanted no part of going one-on-one with Berkowitz. He was intimidating enough in a full classroom.

Berkowitz's office wasn't what I expected: It was immaculate. Berkowitz thanked me for the assignment and ordered me to sit. I apologized again for the mishap, which I immediately regretted.

"Thanks for coming, but please, please don't apologize," he scolded.

"I know. I know. I'll make it better."

"Good. You're learning."

Berkowitz handed me a cup of hot cider and a small maple donut.

"They're fresh," he said. "We don't do bagels at North South, but we're spectacular at donuts.

"How are your parents?" he asked.

"They're fine," I answered succinctly.

Berkowitz sensed my reticence.

"I get it. They can be a bit much," Berkowitz said cheerfully. "But they're supposed to be. They're parents. You should've met my parents. They were hall of fame annoying, Olympic quality."

As Berkowitz laughed at himself, I sipped my cider.

"Have you ever noticed that certain people laugh out loud at themselves and others don't? What's up with that?" he asked. "It's just something to think about. . . . Or not."

I pondered that for a moment. Berkowitz, Mr. Randolph, and my mother laughed out loud at themselves. Wally, Rosemary, and my father didn't. Wally did smile all the time though.

"That's interesting. I never thought about that."

"Well, that's why we're here: to think. I'm doing my job. At least that's what I tell myself."

I bit into the donut. Immediately, I wanted another, which is the problem with donuts. It was delicious, unlike anything, and it was gone in seconds.

"There's some pepper in there, and that gives some kick," explained Berkowitz. "Are you enjoying North South?"

"It's going well."

"You're evading the question Mr. Mills. Do you like it?"

"I'm a little homesick."

"Understandable," Berkowitz replied. "It's a major adjustment, and it's going to take time."

"I was sick of home when I was there."

"Well, here's an exercise for us: Start thinking of North South as your home, which it is. Put the past where it belongs: in the past. Let's live in the moment."

Easier said than done.

"You gave me something to read, so I'm going to return the favor," Berkowitz replied as he reached into his drawer and pulled out a copy of his book *Alone*, which chronicled his experiences in solitary confinement. Before he handed it to me, he quickly jotted something inside.

When I left, I read what Berkowitz had written:

> Dylan:
> You're a first-string goalie in my book.
> MAKE IT BETTER!
> Berkowitz

Berkowitz had read my application. I was a little embarrassed, but I was also proud.

*

No one answered when I knocked on 420, but I could hear Jimmy's guitar and smell incense—at least I think it was incense. When I walked in, there was no smoking taking place, but there was plenty of secondhand smoke. As Jimmy performed, I took a seat on the couch. I started to get that strange calm feeling again.

"You never actually smoke pot, Mills, but you're a pothead!" I imagined Berkowitz yelling. When Jimmy left the room for a break, I sat in front of the keyboard and played one of Barry's best. I played for just a minute—or maybe it was longer. I wasn't quite sure. Everyone was in their private, stoned worlds, and they ignored me, I think, but who knows.

When I collapsed onto my bed, there was a Rosemary text.

How's life? ☺

Yeah, another emoji. I wanted pizza crust. I called. I expected voice mail.

"What's going on?" Rosemary slurred.

Weird. I'd never heard such a phrase from her. She'd had a few, at least.

"I think I'm a little high."

I shouldn't of said it, but after Berkowitz's lying lecture, I was trying to be honest.

"Did you smoke? I hear they got some obscene dope up there."

"No, I didn't smoke."

"Gummy bears?"

I ignored Rosemary's weak attempt at humor. I should've lied! What's one more?

"People were smoking around me."

"Sounds fun. Were there girls there?"

Had I heard correctly?

"What?"

"Were there any gals there?"

Why was Rosemary asking about *gals*?

"No," I answered instinctively.

"There weren't any gals? You're lying!"

Yes, I was.

"I don't know. It was smoky." I was lying again!

"You couldn't tell if there were girls there?"

We both laughed because I was a terrible liar.

"How are those North South gals anyway?"

It was definitely more than a few. Where was this going? There wasn't a good answer. I should've ended the call right then and there. There was no way we were going to define our relationship tonight. Say good night. Now.

But I couldn't. I couldn't say good night to Rosemary.

"Why are you asking me this?"

"I don't know. I'm curious," Rosemary said somewhat curtly.

Before I could answer, Rosemary changed the subject.

"What are you wearing?" she asked.

Where was this going now? Was this standard procedure for long-distance relationships? More importantly, were we even in a long-distance relationship?

Before I could answer, Rosemary asked, "Are you wearing that North South long sleeve?"

She was referring to the same one I was wearing at Luncheonette.

"You mean the one you don't like, right?"

"Honestly, it's not my favorite."

"I have a question for you," I asked, trying to not sound annoyed.

"What? You want to know what I'm wearing?" Rosemary cackled.

"I'm being serious."

"So am I. You're no fun. Ask away, dude."

Dude?

It was a punch to the gut. Rosemary had never referred to me as dude, and it made me feel random, and it pushed me to just come out with it.

"Are you . . . are you embarrassed that I go to North South?"

"You want the truth?" she asked in a very serious voice.

How did things get so tense? I wished I'd never brought it up. I wanted to go back to what we were wearing! But there was no going back.

"You want the truth?" Rosemary repeated.

I wanted to yell for Berkowitz, "NO LIE LIKE EVERYONE ELSE!" Instead, I replied sarcastically, "No, I don't want the truth!"

Rosemary didn't laugh. What happened? Suddenly, I wasn't funny.

"A little," Rosemary quickly answered in almost a whisper. "Well, a little more than a little."

"A little more than a little is a lot!"

"I don't know. Maybe. Are you angry?"

"I'm not angry." I was very angry.

"I just know you can do better. It's a compliment."

"I can't wait to hear an insult."

"I'm sorry."

"Don't be sorry. Make it better!" I demanded angerly.

"Make it better? What are you talking about? You're so high."

"Yes, I'm high," I roared. "I'm North Southed out of my freakin' gourd!"

I was completely sober now, and I was fuming. I didn't know what to say, so I waited. I waited for an apology. And I waited for Rosemary to say she loved me. It was coming.

But it didn't.

Silence.

As I waited for Rosemary's apology, which she was care-fully crafting, I started analyzing. Why was I angry? Rosemary was right. I could do better. I was embarrassed that I went to North South. Why should I be upset that Rosemary was embarrassed?

After a while, Rosemary still hadn't uttered a word. However, I could hear her breathing. Soon Rosemary was snoring, loudly. I lay there listening to her until I passed out.

OCTOBER

There was no us. We were back to no contact. Days came and went. And I went to class, did my work, like I was reporting for a Luncheonette shift. School was my job. But as much as I tried not to, my mind would always rotate back to Rosemary. We'd be biking around Castleton's immaculate streets, swimming underwater in Castleton's empty pool, and singing Barry at the top of our lungs in her car. And yeah, I kept returning to our goalie training and that night after the hockey dance at the gazebo.

> *Do you remember how I remember, Rosemary?*
> *Or am I a forgotten memory?*
> *Where are you, Rosemary?*
> *Where are you?*
> *Rosemary! Rosemary! Rosemary!*

It was over now. Would I ever see Rosemary again?

Of course, we'd see each other again—but it would be super weird and awkward. I thought that was for other people, never us.

Of course, I couldn't surprise Rosemary for her birthday. I would cancel my flight. I just hadn't gotten around to it—story of my life. I didn't want to leave my closet. Besides class, I didn't do much else. I told Quarters that I couldn't attend vert disc practice because of my ankle. It was a lie. Even if I had two good ankles, I wouldn't have gone. And I never bothered to audition for North South's a cappella group.

It wasn't all bad. My happy essay had inspired a Berkowitz lecture—or rather challenge.

"When we say 'whatever,' it's the easy way out—a shortcut," yelled Berkowitz. "Take the time to say what you mean. Never say 'whatever'—ever!"

Berkowitz didn't stop there.

Whenever we heard someone—anyone—utter "whatever," Berkowitz directed us to interview that person and find out what was really on their mind.

"We will find out some interesting things," Berkowitz promised. "They're hiding something, and they might not even know it."

An aggressive knock at my door shook me from myself.

"It's Berkowitz!" growled a gruff voice. Berkowitz was known to show up at dorm rooms unannounced. Somehow, he knew but how?

"Open up, Mr. Mills!"

It wasn't Berkowitz.

"Duuude, where are you?" Wally blared in his funny, Wally way.

"I'm lying low."

"You're what? Talk to me." I nodded to my desk chair, offering him a seat.

"But not here. It's claustrophobic. You got to open the windows or something." I was dining in in my closet, and it was starting to reek.

I wound up treating Wally to sundaes at North South's Ice Cream Factory, which manufactured its ice cream from scratch, and I confessed: Rosemary and I weren't speaking or texting or anything. We were done. I didn't mention anything about Rosemary being embarrassed that I went to North South. Wally was very proud of North South, and I didn't want to insult him.

As I walked back to my closet, I felt a little better. The ice cream and talking helped—but it also hurt. It made me face a new reality I didn't want to face: Rosemary had moved on.

Suddenly, my phone rang. It was a text.

Rosemary.

Yes.

> When we spoke the other night, I was wasted, and I think I said some things that were way out of line. I'm truly sorry. Please accept my apology.

I didn't respond immediately. I wanted the right response, and I wanted Rosemary to wait, just like she'd made me wait. I did what my father always told me not to do: play games.

Two days later, I texted her these two words.

> Apology accepted.

Add another lie to my long list. Rosemary's apology wasn't accepted. As much as I didn't want to be, I was still pissed. And I was just as upset with myself as I was with Rosemary. Rosemary was right. I could've been better. I had every advantage. My parents had groomed me for greatness. When I wasn't, I slipped and settled into mediocrity.

I kept telling myself to cancel my flight, but I just never pulled the trigger. If she hadn't sent that apology, I would've done it by now, at least that's what I told myself. After a week of sparse, emoji-riddled texts, I was awoken by a late-night text.

> I know that things have been kind of weird between us.

Us! Yes, that was the word I wanted to hear.

But I don't want them to be. I hope you enjoy this.

Rosemary sent along a link. I didn't open it immediately. Finally, I took a deep breath and dove in. It was a video. Rosemary was sitting in her enormous dorm room, and she was singing in her off-key voice, which was hilarious.

> *Let's make a date.*
> *I wanna go to Mars with you.*
> *Just you and me.*
> *Let's be what we can truly be.*
> *I wanna go to Mars with you.*
> *We gotta go.*
> *It'll be quite a show.*
> *Please don't say no.*
> *I wanna go to Mars with you.*

I trembled. I smiled. I would've danced if my closet weren't so small.

Rosemary wanted to go to Mars with me!

Yeah, I know that neither of us were going to Mars, but it was the thought. I'd written the thing for her on Valentine's Day senior year. Everything was in the past. I needed to see Rosemary, and Rosemary needed to see me. Finally.

*

It was the day—finally. I was surprising Rosemary for her birthday. I had a late afternoon plane. After class, I endured one of Wally's brutal bodyweight workouts. After my ankle felt better, I started working out with him. Yeah, I preferred that over sharing a joint. Definitely. During box jumps, I landed awkwardly on my bad ankle, and my workout abruptly ended. Under normal circumstances, it would've hurt like hell. But not today, because today was the day.

I still had a few hours, so I limped over to the library to do some reading. There was no shortage of that. I often felt that the North South professors were trying to prove something by assigning so much. I guess we all had something to prove. In case you're wondering, Berkowitz assigned the least. Studying in the library was good in theory. In reality, it was a disaster.

As I attempted to bury myself in history, I noticed Sam conversing with someone. Besides a few nods as we hurried to class, we hadn't had much interaction. I stood behind her, maybe twelve feet away, and waited. She probably saw me but maybe not. After a few minutes, I took a seat in the aisle, so she'd have to pass me on her way out. I kept one eye on her and one eye on history. Surprise, no history was getting done. Finally, I decided to buckle down and put two eyes on history. Sam couldn't miss me. But just as the War of 1812 got its hooks into me, I glimpsed Sam missing me. I ran after her.

"What are you doing?" I asked.

"I'm getting out of here," she replied in a lukewarm voice. "I've been here too long, and I need some air."

"I'm sorry I missed the scrimmage."

Right after I said it, I thought of Berkowitz.

"You should be. But you can make it up this weekend. We have another."

"I can't."

"What ya got?"

"I'm surprising Rosemary for her birthday."

"She doesn't know you're coming?"

"No, not a clue, but she loves surprises. She gave me a surprise birthday party last year."

"Well, have a great trip. I've gotta run."

Sam was nonchalant, as if she couldn't care less. I didn't want her to care, well, maybe a little. Was that wrong?

Wally gave me a ride to the airport on the back of his motorcycle. Right after I got on, I regretted not taking an Uber. Wally's a madman on the road, and there were some hilly, twisting narrow roads on Wally's back-roads shortcut. For the entire one-hour and ten-minute ride, which Wally somehow maneuvered in fifty-six minutes, I shut my eyes and held on to Wally for dear life. When we arrived at the airport, my eyes were tearing, and I was completely numb. I walked through the airport bowlegged.

Wally escorted me to security, where there wasn't a single person in line. Before I went through, we looked at each other for a moment, acknowledging that something momentous was ahead. He was wearing one of TTK's acorn necklaces, which I'd given him. We embraced quickly, and I went through the detector. After I was cleared, I glanced back. Wally hadn't moved, still smiling. I waved and turned the corner toward the boarding area. I was on my way.

And then I wasn't.

There was a delay, at least an hour, something about heavy rain in Chicago or maybe it was Cleveland. Dad would've been all over that weather stuff. I wasn't. I picked up Berkowitz's *Eavesdropping* but put it down. I tried not to think about Sam and how I pissed her off. I tried not to think about why I wanted her to care just a little. I nervously paced the boarding area, downed three overpriced waters, and relieved myself maybe eight or nine times. I lost count. Nerves.

There was no waiting on the runway, and the two-hour and thirty-five-minute flight arrived early. As I sat waiting to land, I planned the evening's itinerary: Rosemary and I would grab a late dinner or maybe just dessert, though neither of us were really dessert people unless it involved Luncheonette's white chocolates. Or maybe we'd get a beer or two, though beer wasn't me. But it wasn't about me. It was about Rosemary. If Rosemary wanted to smoke dope, we'd smoke dope. Yeah, Rosemary would call the shots, just like old times.

As soon as the seat belt sign went off, I rushed off the plane with my backpack and my bouquet of roses that somehow survived Wally's hell ride and shimmied around grumbling passengers as they unloaded their carry-ons from their overheads. I dashed through the airport and ran in front of a cab. I was perspiring. It was much warmer here, downright tropical. When the driver asked me where to, I panicked: I didn't know the name of Rosemary's dorm. She'd texted me an image, but I didn't have the name, and all of the gothic buildings at Rosemary's school looked identical. It was just another thing I didn't know about Rosemary.

The cab driver dropped me off in front of Einstein's Alley, a castle, where a lot of the freshman lived. Rosemary's school would make the perfect setting for a medieval festival. I tried to enter, but the door required a security card

"Do you know Rosemary Silversmith?" I asked two guys in matching khaki shorts and golf lids.

"Who?" one of them asked, barely looking at me, not breaking stride.

"Rosemary Silversmith. She's a freshman," I explained as I ran after him. "She's the hockey team manager."

They barely shook their heads and kept going. Next, I spotted two girls in very expensive workout attire and yoga mats heading inside. They were just a few yards from the door, so I had to hustle, and I wound up tripping on the curb and into a puddle. I didn't fall, but I muddied myself. Just after the girls entered, I grabbed the door, but I was a microsecond too late. It was locked. I sat outside Einstein's Alley, dejected and dirty.

Maybe this trip was a mistake, another.

And then someone left the dorm, and I simply grabbed the open door before it shut and walked in. Maybe this trip wasn't a mistake. I asked a few students if they knew

Rosemary, but no one did. After I'd gone through the first floor, I walked up to the second, which was empty. I took off my soiled button-down. Just as I was about to put on my North South T-shirt, I was approached by a man who looked like a grad student, and a security guard.

"Excuse me, sir. Can we help you?" asked the grad student. He was really saying, "I don't want to help you. Please leave." It didn't help my case that I was shirtless. At least I was a little buff thanks to Wally's workouts. I looked more like a hockey player now than when I was almost a hockey player.

"I'm looking for Rosemary Silversmith. She's my girlfriend, and she's a freshman here."

"Do *you* go to school here?" the grad student asked accusingly.

"No. I just flew in. I know I'm a mess. I tripped outside."

"Are you sure she's in Einstein's Alley?"

"No."

"Which dorm is she in?"

"I'm not sure."

"You don't know the name of your girlfriend's dorm?"

"No, it's complicated. Freshman year has been really, really weird."

Yeah, it was an understatement.

"If you're not a student here or a guest of a resident, you cannot be here," said the security guard. "You're trespassing."

Suddenly, I was back in Castleton.

I just started walking aimlessly as if I'd somehow miraculously bump into Rosemary. Rosemary's campus is often described as one of the most beautiful in the country. Yeah, it's immaculate, just like Castleton. I felt like I could eat off its pavement. But it was too nice, artificial. Perhaps I was too quick to judge. Yeah, I had some Castleton in me, born and bred. I'd just arrived. Maybe this place would grow on me.

Maybe my grades would rock at North South, and maybe I'd transfer here so we could be us 2.0. Maybe.

"You can't live on maybes. I want definites!" I heard my father bark at me.

There would be no surprise. I wanted a definite. I finally broke down and called Rosemary. Straight to voice mail. No message. I texted Dorian. Dorian had friends everywhere, including Rosemary's *it* school. Minutes later, Dorian texted me the name of Rosemary's dorm, Newcomb's Secret, as well as her room number. I was just steps away from Newcomb's Secret when my phone rang. Rosemary. I didn't bother looking at the caller ID.

"What are you up to?" Dorian asked suspiciously.

"I'm surprising Rosemary for her birthday," I replied triumphantly as I entered Newcomb's Secret. A student had opened the door for me, or rather he didn't stop me.

"Where are you?" Dorian asked.

"I'm at Rosemary's dorm!" I answered as I ran up to Rosemary's room on the third floor.

"Why are you running?"

I wasn't listening. I knocked on Rosemary's door, but no one answered. I knocked again and again, still no answer. "Rosemary's not here!"

"Are you guys still seeing other people?"

"I was never seeing other people!"

"Is Rosemary?"

I was stung, just the thought . . .

"I don't think so," I managed to reply. "No."

No, Rosemary wasn't seeing other people, of course not. The girl wanted to go to Mars with me!

"You never told me . . ." I wasn't listening—again. I kept waiting for Rosemary to open the door.

"Dylan Mills!"

Dorian had my attention. Whenever Dorian addressed me by my full name, something was going down. "If I tell you something, do you promise to not be mad at me?"

At least I think that's what she said. I heard her but I didn't want to. Answer the door Rosemary!

"Why would I be mad at you?"

"Well, after I texted her, my friend called. And . . ."

Nothing good usually comes after *and*—but I bit.

"And what?" Dorian wouldn't answer, which made me a little insane. "AND WHAT?"

"I don't know if this is true, but she told me that Rosemary is . . . seeing someone."

"What are you talking about?"

"You promised you wouldn't be mad at me."

"I LIED! You got misinformation. I got to go."

"Dylan don't."

"Don't what? I'm surprising Rosemary for her birthday. Thank you for your help. You're a great friend. I love you!"

I yelled it like we were mortal enemies.

*

I frantically rushed down to Newcomb's Secret's lounge, where I aggressively interrogated a few students on Rosemary's whereabouts.

"She might be at one of the supper clubs," sneered a kid with a blue blazer and obnoxious, ruby-colored three-quarters-length shorts. Rosemary's school called their fraternities supper clubs. "Who are you?"

"Who are *you*?" I snapped back.

As I stormed out, I overheard some of the students talking.

"Was that a North South shirt he had on?" someone snidely remarked.

"Yeah," said another. "I hear they got good weed up there."

On cue, I did a 180.

"North South's weed isn't good," I yelled. "IT'S THE BEST WEED IN THE WORLD!"

I stormed out again. They probably called security. I would've.

My phone kept vibrating.

Dorian.

She'd called five or six times. I wouldn't answer because I couldn't speak, but I could scream. I needed to find Rosemary. All the fraternities, uh supper houses, whatever they were, looked identical, just like everything on this campus, including the people. Money looks the same. This school had something against freckles. I waited in line at the first supper house I bumped into. They were checking IDs at the door, and I showed them my goofy passport.

"Are you planning on going abroad?" smirked the guy at the door as he handed me a red wrist band. I charged through the basement, where there was lame, uninspired dancing. I hurried through the place like a loon, quickly scanning the room's faces.

No Rosemary.

I got the same result at the next house and was refused entry at the one after because they were overcapacity. I surrendered, again. I called Rosemary.

Voice mail again.

No message. I hadn't a clue what would come out of my mouth. I'll tell you one thing about these so-called supper clubs: They weren't serving any food, which sucked because I was starving.

By midnight, I'd lost track of how many houses I'd visited. After one house looked at me, or more specifically my North South shirt, and told me that they weren't accepting any more guests, I had enough. I walked around the house's backyard, where I spotted a hammock and laid down in it. Well, I would've, but I didn't lay in the hammock's sweet spot, and it wound up immediately flipping me over and on to the ground, where I just lay, trying to ignore the echo of the annoying generic pop from the stupid supper club. As I lay there, I couldn't ignore a pair of female voices from the first floor.

"He's so hot."

"I know. I know."

"Do you think he thinks I'm hot?"

"Definitely."

"I just hope he's not too hot for me."

I walked toward the voices because, well, I wanted to judge how hot she was for myself. They were in the supper club's restroom, and the window was open. But when I pulled myself up to the ledge, the restroom was empty.

Suddenly, I had a gut feeling: Rosemary was here!

With surprisingly little effort, I was in the supper club's lady's room. It was almost too easy. Just as I finished washing my face, two girls walked in.

"Why are you here?" one yelled.

"I'm—"

"There's a creepy guy in here. Could someone help us!" the other yelled before I could answer.

"I just wanted to wash up. Don't—"

"Get out of here you perv!"

After the p word was uttered, I panicked and climbed back out the window. As easily as I'd entered, I exited. But when I hit the ground, I had company: about a dozen drunken guys who were looking for any excuse to pummel someone.

"I was just trying to surprise my girlfriend," I blabbered repeatedly. I was too pathetic to beat up.

As they drove me off campus, campus security told me that I was getting off with a warning. If I returned, I would be promptly arrested. They were nice enough to drop me off at a diner. Their French fries were soggy, but I scarfed them like they were the best thing ever. I also recharged my phone, which had died. In the bathroom, I cleaned up and put on my North South sweatshirt. It had gotten a bit cooler. I was ready to go—where I didn't know. And then my phone rang.

"Where are you?" I asked before Rosemary could say a word.

"Where are you?"

"I'm here at your school, well just off campus. It's a long story."

After a pause, Rosemary asked, "Why?"

No, this wasn't the greeting I was looking for.

"I'm here to surprise you for your birthday. You love surprises."

"Well that's so thoughtful, but—" Uh oh, I got the *but*, and I braced myself. "I wish you would've told me."

"Then it wouldn't have been a surprise."

"Can you come to my dorm?"

"Well, I can't. I was banned from campus."

"You were what? Why?"

"It doesn't matter. You know I really don't care if they arrest me. I care about you. I'm coming to you!"

I tossed some money on the table and got up to leave to see Rosemary.

"Arrest? What are you talking about?"

"Who cares!? I'm on my way."

"Dylan, there's something I need to tell you."

"There's something I need to tell you: I've missed you so much and I LOVE YOU!"

Silence.

"Are you there?" I yelled.

More silence.

"Dylan, I can't talk about this now."

"Talk about what?"

"You're acting crazy!" Rosemary shouted.

"You're making me crazy!" I shouted even louder.

"Dylan . . . ," she paused. "I'm seeing someone."

My heart was beating out of my chest.

"What do you mean you're seeing someone?"

"You know."

"No, I don't know."

"I'm seeing someone."

I was about to vomit.

"For how long?"

"Not long."

"How long?"

"Dylan, we agreed to see other people."

"Yeah, and you told me that you wanted to go to Mars with me. How can we go to Mars if we're seeing other people? Mars doesn't work that way."

"It's just a song, Dylan."

"I know. It's just a song. I wrote the song." Why did I write that song? "Look, I don't care. I'm coming over."

"You shouldn't. You'll get arrested."

"I told you. I don't care."

"You shouldn't."

"Why do you keep telling me to not come over when I'm here? Why?"

"Because . . . ."

"Why do you keep pausing?"

"Because he just walked into the room."

*

I had no destination, but I started running as fast as I could. Why was I still holding the roses? When I couldn't run anymore, I leaned over and almost threw up the soggy fries.

After I'd regained some sense of composure, I sat on the concrete and called Dorian.

"I'm an idiot. I'm sorry."

"I'm sorry, Dylan."

I wept quietly until I couldn't. Dorian asked if I wanted to stay at her friend's. I declined. I couldn't be around anyone, and no one could be around me. And I wanted out of here as soon as possible. I needed to return home.

North South.

I gladly paid the flight change fee and managed to get a 7:45 a.m. flight, but it had *four* transfers. Even though I was the first in line, security was a major hassle. The TSA agents were convinced that I was trouble, or maybe they just needed something to do. If they were smart, they would've pegged me as a drug courier. But they weren't. Instead, they took me to a private room.

"What's the name of your school?" one of the security guys badgered.

"North South," I answered.

"Which is it: North or South?" he said.

"It's both."

"What kind of name is that?"

"It's a ridiculous name."

It was kind of ridiculous and funny, but these dimwits couldn't find funny with a GPS.

"If you don't cut it out, we'll lock you up!"

After an extensive background check, I was finally cleared. At the near-empty boarding area, I charged my phone, which had run out of juice shortly after I'd hung up with Dorian. I sprawled out on the airport's carpeted floor, shut my eyes, and imagined a world where a time machine existed, so I could erase the previous night—or the previous two years.

I regretted ever meeting Rosemary Silversmith.

But I still desperately wanted her to call me.

After I charged my phone, a text from Rosemary popped up.

Rosemary had come to her senses.

Late is better than never. It's a blessing that time machines didn't exist. It had arrived four minutes after 1:00.

    Dylan

Well, we were off to a terrible start. She was using my full name, never a good sign.

    So sorry about how this turned out.

No! Don't say sorry. Make it better!

    Thank you so much for making the trip.

Please never thank me again. I'm not filling your water glass at Luncheonette.

        I can arrange for a place for you to stay. Some of the hockey dudes live off campus, and they said you can crash on their couch. They're super cool. Let me know.

Yes, that would be super cool: to be a burden on the super cool hockey dudes. We're not a good fit. I'm not cool. I'm into Barry! There, I said it! I'm a glee club dropout, and I was the fifth-string goalie. And as long as we're setting the record straight, I was a bold-faced liar. My biggest lie was the one I told myself: that Rosemary and I had a chance.

*

I'd messed up, again. When I took a close look at my syllabi, I was alarmed to find that I had a geology exam in a few days, which counted for 35 percent of my grade. As much as I vowed to stay on top of things, I hadn't, at least with geology. I let things get away from me, again. I'd wanted geology to disappear. Yeah, ignoring it only made it worse. I caught up on the reading, but I wasn't feeling it for rocks. If I didn't do something drastic, I was going to fail.

    Wally.

Vocabulary wasn't Wally's thing, but he owned rocks. I went to 420 and asked—okay, begged—him to tutor me. I didn't have to beg too hard.

"I'll get you ready for this," Wally said confidently. "It's a guarantee."

"How do you know?"

"It's rocks. It's not rocket science."

Wally wound up getting really got into it, utilizing about a hundred cue cards to quiz me with relentlessly.

On Sunday night, we got some chowder at North South's campus restaurant. As we slurped, Wally quizzed me like a drill sergeant.

"You need to know this in your sleep," he demanded. Afterwards, we returned to 420. Wally ordered me to write a song about rocks. I wrote a horrible, horrible song, but it helped. After a few days of this, I was as ready as I was going to be.

But on the night before the test, I got anxious. When I didn't want to sleep, I crashed instantly. When I needed to pass out, I couldn't. I poked around Instagram and checked up on the Castleton crew. I knew this was treacherous water, but I swam anyway. It was usually kids at their *it* schools; no photoshopping necessary. In addition to the acorn necklaces, TTK was now selling sunflower bouquets for $100 a pop.

"You can always count on the sun," TTK wrote. I thought, "You can't at North South." It seemed like we got one sunny day a week, if that. I bought one anyway. It looked like Dorian had a few pictures of herself smiling with a new guy. I think she was on her third. I'd lost count. Why couldn't I just pass out?

Kody's Instagram had weirdly vanished. Rosemary didn't post much on Instagram, but I checked anyway. Surprise: Rosemary had posted. There was a football stadium shot at sunrise. Rosemary loved Calm Lake sunrises. I guess sunrises anywhere would do. In another, she was posing with four girlfriends, none of whom I knew anything about. At first glance, they looked like an eclectic group. But when I looked closer, I saw they were practically the same: conservative, expensive jeans and fancy T-shirts; all radiating affluence. Next, Rosemary was posing with four hockey dudes in their jerseys on the ice rink. Were these the dudes she wanted me to bunk with? They were tall and dark, and their hair seemed to fall just right over their foreheads, no, not a freckle in sight. They looked like Castleton hockey players, just older and bigger. I knew one thing for certain: Rosemary was done with freckles. Which one of these guys was Rosemary's guy? I studied each one. It was futile. These guys could've been quadruplets.

She wrote underneath the photo:

> Looking forward to lots of goals and reaching our goals.

It was just a picture, but it was for the universe. I couldn't stop staring. Finally, I turned off my phone. I closed my eyes and pleaded with myself to pass out.

But I couldn't. And I couldn't help myself.

I turned my phone back on. Off. On. I stared down each of these hockey dudes until I couldn't stare anymore.

Suddenly, I was back in Castleton, sitting at Luncheonette, taking my geology test. As usual, it was packed, but no one was eating or religiously checking their phones. The Luncheonette's brunchers were taking bong hits. Mr. and Mrs. Z were on each side of me, one riding each ear.

"It's useless. You should just give up!" Mr. Z screamed as smoke billowed everywhere. "Give up and just bus tables for the rest of your life!"

I got maybe four restless hours of sleep. Before the test, Wally and I met at 7:00 for coffee. Wally immediately sensed something wasn't right.

"What's wrong, duuude?" he asked.

"I didn't get much sleep."

"You love to sleep. You're an honor roll sleeper. What happened?"

"Instagram."

"You're not on Instagram."

"I was Instagram surfing."

"Was it surfing or stalking?"

I didn't reply.

"Not good, not good at all," Wally said disapprovingly, as he checked his watch. "Well, we still got some time."

Wally whipped out his cue cards, and suddenly we were back to quizzing.

"It's official: My brain's inside your brain," Wally declared when we were done.

I laughed, but then I thought, "It's good that my brain isn't inside your brain because you'd be consumed with Rosemary and the stupid quadruplets."

There were sixty-five multiple-choice questions on the test. I finished in exactly forty-eight minutes. I trusted my gut and didn't go over my answers. Second-guessing would lead to third- and fourth-guessing and I'd never finish. When I handed in my test, most of the class was still at it. Wally was already gone, no surprise. As I walked out of the lecture hall, I felt twenty pounds lighter. Whatever happened, happened, but I don't think I failed. I think I did okay, even decent. I don't want to get ahead of myself. Either way, it was over. I was elated, but I was also exhausted. I returned to my closet to collapse. As usual, just when I wanted to, I couldn't. Instead, I stared at Rosemary's photo.

Why was it still up? Better question: Why couldn't I take it down? Just a few moments ago, I was sky-high. Now I was down. I had to do something. I had to live in the present, just like Berkowitz prescribed. Sadly, Rosemary was the past.

Just as I was about to toss it, Wally showed. As he entered, I placed the photo in a cardboard box.

"How'd it go?"

"I don't want to jinx it. Thanks for pulling me through."

"You were making me study too."

"Why don't you come to the gym with me?" Wally offered.

"I'm beat, and I got some reading."

"Yeah, there's always reading," Wally groaned as he stood in my doorway for a moment, contemplating.

"Can you do me a favor?"

"What's up?"

"Could you hold this box for me?"

"What's this?"

"It's nothing."

"If it were anyone else, I'd think it was weed."

"It's Rosemary's photo," I said glumly. Wally looked at the open space on my desk. "It's distracting. And—"

"Say no more. I'll keep it in a safe place. You'll probably get back together and then you'll want it back."

*

I started Shakespeare's *As You Like It* for Hammer. I know everything's based on Shakespeare, but it doesn't go down easy. I read half a scene, fell asleep for ten minutes, and read another quarter before my mind drifted. I can't completely blame Shakespeare. Rosalind is one of the protagonists in *As You Like It*.

Rosalind. Rosemary. Rosalind.

I missed Rosemary's photo. It'd been a friend. I had a lot of heart-to-hearts with that photo. It's not that odd. When you think about it, people often say the same stuff repeatedly. I'd instructed Wally to put the photo in a safe place, far away from Sherbert, and to not return it. But now, after just a few days, I was yearning for it. I didn't request it back, but I did something far worse. I returned to Rosemary's Instagram.

And there were new photos.

I cringed. Before I examined them closely, I found the strength to turn off my phone. I shouldn't look. I waivered. I shouldn't look, but I did, and I got smacked with Rosemary and him. They were standing in front of yet another gothic fortress. Caption:

> When you're at the perfect school with the perfect guy.

Can't you find a synonym for "perfect"? How about "ideal"? I guess that doesn't work.

I wasn't the perfect guy, or anywhere close, but Rosemary used to tell me I was. Rosemary should've said I was the perfect guy for the moment. I kept telling myself to shut my phone down. But then there was another urgent voice that wanted to know what Rosemary was up to.

Rosemary and her perfect guy were tailgating at a football game, holding plastic cups.

> Cheers to football Saturday.

Why are you cheering to football, Rosemary? You're hockey all the way. Who are you? They were dressed in ridiculous formal wear, with heels.

> Ready to dance at Sunday formals!

What are Sunday formals? How can you dance in those absurd stilts? Rosemary hated stilts! She just wasn't that type of girl. At least, I thought she wasn't that type of girl.

My phone rang.

Text. Rosemary?

It wasn't. It never was. It was a reminder from North South Athletics that the women's team had a game in ninety minutes. I'd already been to a few scrimmages. It was fun, and I got to watch Sam make someone look stupid other than myself. I cleaned up nice. Yeah, it was about time.

North South was renovating its gymnasium, so the team played at the town's rec center. I sat in the corner of the bleachers, my usual spot. The few people there got to see a pretty good game. When Sam and her teammates, many of whom I'd met and danced with, pulled away in the final ten minutes, I started to play my own game: the what-if game, yeah, a very dangerous game.

What if I'd allowed myself to see other people?

What if I'd taken Sam out to dinner with my parents when they visited?

What if I hadn't gotten that phone call from Rosemary that night?

What if I hadn't run home that weekend?

What if I didn't push Sam away?

There are no do-overs, but I wanted one. I started to strategize about Sam. I imagined our post-game conversation.

"Great game," I'd say.

"Thanks and thanks for coming," she'd reply.

"What are you up to?"

"I don't know."

"Do you wanna get something to eat?"

"Like a date?"

"Definitely a date."

"So you're seeing other people?"

"No," I'd reply smoothly. "Just you."

It was an incredible conversation, but, of course, it was 100 percent fantasy.

After the game, I waited in the corner of the rec center's lobby. When Sam emerged from the locker room, she was glowing from the intense physical activity, and her short hair was still wet from showering. As she stood in place checking her phone, I started toward her.

Operation Sam was in motion.

But just as I made my approach, a guy tapped her on the shoulder and embraced her, in not a friend-zone sort of way. Immediately, I did an about-face and walked quickly in the opposite direction, feeling foolish and, yeah, jealous.

NOVEMBER

A nd I was bad, very bad. Because I was doing what I shouldn't be doing, again, ever: Instagram stalking.

I could lock myself away and keep myself awake for days doing this. But after less than a few seconds, I'd had enough. In this one, that guy was dressed in his hockey practice gear.

> When you meet your soul mate, anything seems possible. Even Mars feels within reach.

No! I know that no one's going to Mars, but if anyone were going, it was supposed to be me, and I was going to persuade you to come.

Mars was out of bounds.

I was sad. I was infuriated. I furiously paced in my closet, but there wasn't enough space to pace, so I went out to the hallway. I had my dark blue Castleton hockey hat pulled tightly over my head down to my eyes. I looked like a lunatic. I was a lunatic. I paced past 420. I could hear Jimmy playing, and I walked in without knocking. Wally was tapping on his bongos, smiling as usual. Some of the usual suspects were also there. I didn't know much about them, and they probably knew less about me. I'd been away for two weekends, and when I was at North South, I wasn't. I was locked in my closet wondering when or if Rosemary would ever text again, listening to the Walkman she gave me. Jimmy and I nodded at one another, and I dove right in. I think this is what I yelled, but I can't be sure.

> *We're not going to Mars! No! No!*
> *We're not going. We're not going.*
> *We're not going to Mars! No! No!*

Everyone was into it, nodding and shaking their fists. Who knows if they had a clue of what I was saying. They were probably wasted on Sherbert's dope. When I was done, I was soaked in perspiration. Dandruff girl handed me a shot and a beer, and I downed them like I imagined a real man would—as opposed to a fake man. It was a first for me, the shot. But I immediately regretted it. It felt worse than those gummy bears. Instantly, I became light-headed, eyes watery. For a moment, I felt a gummy bears episode coming on.

But it passed.

I'd done a shot, and now that I'd done it, I was finished with shots—forever.

Some of the crew said they were going uptown. I was all in. We hit Fat Nancy's, but it was too mellow. No one was dancing except Wally. It was fun laughing with him. After two Special Blends, we took off. We hit Porch. I was hoping that Sam and her teammates would be there, but they weren't.

We bumped into a few people from Hammer's class. A film major said he was interested in making a documentary about my parents. He wanted to call it *Happy Divorce*. I told him that I'd ask them. I lied. I wouldn't. I was the only one who was going to exploit my parents' dysfunction. I talked about Berkowitz with a few people for a while. Even though most stayed clear of his class, everyone was fascinated with him.

"Did he really teach a class on death row?" someone asked. He might've. As I was pondering Berkowitz telling doomed men to make it better, Wally grabbed me.

"We got to get out of here," he said. "We need something with more character."

We wound up at an after-hours in a dark basement at Society, North South's underground motorcycle club. There were lots of black T-shirts, tattoos, and Timberlands. All of the girls seemed to be wearing bright red lipstick. Punk pop was crankin'. Sam wasn't here, nor would I expect her to be. It wasn't her scene. It wasn't my scene. I didn't know anyone, but a few were familiar with my parents.

"When are they coming back?" a cute, short girl with short black hair slurred. A few guys and one enormous woman pumped a keg in the corner, filling sixteen-ounce plastic mugs. Wally got two and handed me one. A new, unfamiliar song with a thundering bass came on.

"Is this a frat?" I asked Wally.

North South didn't have fraternities, or supper clubs, but maybe there was a loophole or something that I was unaware of.

"Is what fat?" Wally yelled.

"Never mind," I yelled back.

We raised our mugs and drank good beer, at least it tasted good in the moment.

Yeah, I was getting North Southed.

When the music switched over to some disco, a strobe light came on, and everyone started dancing. Wally was in the center of it, as usual, smiling. After a few songs, Wally and some girl pulled me into their dancing circle, and after a song or two, I let loose—until the music abruptly stopped. I figured that the night was over, and I headed for the stairwell, but Wally stopped me.

"The party's just getting started," he whispered, his eyes aglow.

Everyone moved to one side of the basement except for a few guys, who laid down a long, thick plastic sheet, about ten yards. After they poured beer on the sheet and placed twelve plastic cups of beer at the end of it near the wall, classical piano came on over the loudspeakers. Moments later, a few guys in only their boxers emerged, and everyone started counting down. I joined in at five, though I didn't know what I was counting down to. When we got to one, one of the boxer guys dove headfirst onto the sheet and slid. Beer sprayed everywhere, and he crashed into the cups of beer and the wall, which had been padded with rubber rafts.

"Strike!" everyone yelled. After the cups were replaced and refilled, another guy in boxers went. And then another, and another. Most went feetfirst. The guy who lost his boxers mid-slide got the loudest ovation. As he retrieved his soaked boxers from the beer puddle, he didn't bother to cover his privates. When it was Wally's turn, he swayed his hands back and forth like a conductor, smiling the entire time, before taking the plunge. Strike!

After Wally was done, a dozen or so girls filed into the basement in their underwear, led by the enormous woman from the keg. I was surprised, but no one else seemed to be, and the girls were just as gung ho as the guys, if not more. Two or three lost their tops during the slide and subsequent crash. At first I was embarrassed for them, but they weren't. They pumped their fists victoriously and I did too. They were having fun. It was fun.

When there was a lull in the action, a chant started.

"Take it off! Take it off!" I joined in when I figured out what they were saying. "Take it off!" I screamed. The small girl who had asked about my parents came over and stood on her toes so I could hear her. Like everyone else, she was in her underwear and completely drenched.

"What's up bro!" I was caught off guard. I don't recall ever being referred to as bro by a girl. "We're chanting for you to take it off."

"Who, me?" I asked.

"Yeah, you!" she declared, pointing her finger at my chest.

"My ankle's iffy," I explained. "Recovering from a sprain."

"It looked pretty good when you were dancing up a storm," she said with a pouty face. "Don't be shy."

"I'm not shy!" I was shy.

I scanned the dark, sudsy basement. I was the last and only person clothed. I was embarrassed, but if I got undressed, I'd be more embarrassed.

I had a secret, a small one.

I had on my tighty-whities—yeah, nut huggers. At the end-of-summer sale, my mother got a deluxe pack for "a song." Truthfully, it was a wise purchase. Tighty-whities are underrated. They offer tremendous support. But my tighty-whities are not for public consumption. Now with the entire room chanting, I couldn't just walk out and let Wally down. It was a new era; yes, another. I'd been through so many eras, I felt like a science fiction character.

When the chant died, the disco returned. I was already North Southed, but I needed more courage. I downed what little remained in my mug and tossed it down defiantly.

"Let's dance!" I yelled. If I went slow, I'd back out. When I was down to my tighty-whities, I started to dance, and everyone formed a circle around me. I was stalling. But I'd come too far—and there was no turning back now.

I made a breaststroke motion, requesting that the dance circle part. I stared down the cups of beer and assumed a sprinter's stance. After the countdown, I ran and dove head-first onto the plastic sheet, crashing into the cups.

"Strike!" everyone yelled. After ricocheting off the rubber rafts, I high-fived everyone in the room, and I embraced the enormous woman.

We wound up stumbling on to the sudsy floor. Spontaneously—I'm not quite sure how—we had a moment and smooched. I'm not quite sure how long. I was North

Southed. I was cold, wet, and exhilarated. I slid two more times. Good times. Great times.

*

As Wally and I staggered back to the North Pole, I checked my phone. When you can stay clear of your phone for a few hours, that's the sign of a good party. It was a great party. But now, my tighty-whities were frozen, and my head was spinning. I was completely North Southed—and not in a good way.

"Did she text you?" Wally asked.

"Who?"

"Wilma."

"Who's Wilma?"

"The nice lady you were tongue dancing with a few moments ago."

Just as he said it, my phone rang. Text.

> How are you? Are you staying in and studying? I know you're hitting it pretty hard.

Rosemary?

Why was Rosemary texting me? Did she somehow find out about Wilma? Was reconciliation on her mind?

I couldn't sleep, and it was turning light. I could see the sun starting to peek out. Who knows the last time I saw the sun. It was a special occasion. North South was perpetually cloudy. I headed out toward the lake to watch the sunrise. Rosemary and I had seen a few. I took a picture of the sun rising behind the lake. It was *it* school worthy, and I texted it to Rosemary. It was a sunrise pic, but I was also sending a message: This is a new beginning—for *us*.

But I didn't stop with the picture. I scribbled a few lines.

Sunrise in the east.
North South's view is a beast.
It's quite a view.
But much better with you.

I reread it. No, of course, I wouldn't send this. I was going overboard. I deleted it.

Well, I thought I deleted it.

Accidentally, I hit send. Major oops. It was out. I couldn't do anything about it now. I shut my eyes, and I was gone.

But not for long.

My phone was ringing. A legit, 100 percent ring—not a text. My eyes opened into the glaring sun. I answered without checking the number.

"Hello!"

"Dylan?" Rosemary seemed concerned—but distant. It was not a new beginning voice. "Is everything okay?"

"Everything's great," I replied unconvincingly. "Why?"

"You're texting me so early. Were you up all night?"

"Were you up all night?" I almost replied.

"You don't have to tell me if you don't want to."

"I have no secrets. I went to a few bars, and then I went to an after-hours at North South's motorcycle club."

"After-hours at a motorcycle club?"

"It's like a sailing club, except motorcycles," I explained.

"Why didn't you go to the sailing club?"

"I don't sail."

"You don't ride motorcycles."

"I just started."

It just came out. It wasn't necessarily a lie. Sure, I cringed and silently prayed the entire ride that we'd be spared, but I had survived Wally's hell ride.

I plead innocent.

I hadn't planned on mentioning my motorcycle club adventure. But part of me was glad I did. I wanted Rosemary to not think that she knew everything about me. Along the way to mediocrity, sadly, I'd become predictable and boring.

Now, I wanted Rosemary to think that Dylan Mills was dangerous, just a smidge.

"Have you told your parents about this?" Rosemary asked, immediately reminding me that I was anything but dangerous. If I ever got on a motorcycle again, it would probably be on a Vespa with training wheels.

"I don't tell my parents everything." I wanted to add, "Do *you*?" But I restrained myself. I tried to flip the conversation. "How are you?" I asked.

I already knew from Instagram that she was "living her best life."

"Life's good. Thank you for asking," Rosemary replied politely.

Life's good? How much vaguer can you get? I didn't ask her to specify. I didn't want her to. I didn't want to hear about how she was at her *it* school. I needed to say goodbye, quit before it got any worse.

But I couldn't say goodbye to Rosemary.

"Hold on for a sec," Rosemary said. I had had my chance to hang up. Now I was on hold. Rosemary attempted to cover the phone with her hand.

"Who's that?" asked a muffled male voice.

"It's Dylan," I heard Rosemary say.

"Why?" he asked, annoyed. "And why so early?"

He was being logical. I wasn't. And why wouldn't I hang up the phone?

"He was acting strange," Rosemary explained.

"Why should that surprise you?" he sneered. "You told me he's strange."

I'd never hung up on Rosemary. Until now. Rosemary always told me I was kind of strange in an awesome way. She said that she loved it. As I paced in circles, I grimaced. My phone rang. Rosemary. I started to answer, but I stopped myself. I couldn't. Instead, I hurled my phone as far as I could and watched it drop into the lake. It was gone. Yeah, I wanted that time machine again. As I walked back to the North Pole, I thought, "What a strange, stupid thing to do."

*

"Rise and shine, duuuude!" shouted Wally as he stuck his head into my closet. As usual, I was under my lavender comforter surrounded by textbooks. Besides classes and food runs, I hadn't been out much. Weather was brutal. Just today, it had snowed for twenty minutes before turning to sleet. Berkowitz said sleet was God's vomit. I have no recollection of it ever sleeting in Castleton. But horrendous weather had an upside: It helped me stay focused on my studies, which usually was very difficult since I'd made a career of being unfocused. And tossing my phone just might've been my smartest maneuver at North South. Rosemary's Instagram was no longer at my fingertips. Berkowitz somehow got wind of the fact that I'd tossed my phone and was stoked. He even turned it into an assignment, asking everyone to shelve their phones for a week and take notes about their experiences.

"We got somewhere to be," Wally said. "We're going to Society."

"I'm not going back. I can't go back."

"Why? I thought you had fun."

"It was too much fun. And I have reading."

"You can't read all the time. It'll be mellow, promise, and Jimmy's performing."

I was intrigued. I'd never seen Jimmy perform outside of 420.

"I'm in! But I'm not getting naked again!"

"Great! But there's one thing you should know."

"What?"

"Wilma's off the market. She's back with her ex. I told you duuude: You should've texted her."

Society was unrecognizable, the premises and the people. It was spotless—and everyone was fully clothed. A fire was going strong in the upstairs lounge fireplace, and mellow music was playing. Though I didn't really know anyone, everyone treated me as if I were an old friend.

"How could anyone forget the nut hugger duuude?" Wally explained later. I sipped hot cider, which had a sharp bite to it. Wally informed me later that it was spiked with vodka. It went down nice. Before I finished my drink, Jimmy walked to the front and strapped on his guitar. Beside him stood a bassist and a drummer, guys I'd never seen before. Jimmy's trio performed some sedate but intricate instrumentals, nothing like "Satan's School" or anything I'd ever heard from him. The kid was versatile. Between sets, Jimmy sat next to me.

"We could use some vocals?" Jimmy asked after a moment. "You wanna join us?"

I was taken aback. Jimmy had never formally asked me to accompany him. Our 420 sessions were always on the fly. I was welcome, but I was never invited.

I wanted to say, "Hell yes, let's do it!" But I was petrified and not prepared. And yeah, I didn't do solos.

"Can I think about it?" I asked.

I'd already danced in my tighty-whities for this crew. I could do a solo for them.

But I just couldn't pull the trigger.

When I returned to my closet, I wasn't quite North Southed, but I was feeling the spiked cider, and I was frustrated with myself for not taking Jimmy up on his offer. I got under my lavender comforter and scribbled some words down.

All's rearranged.
Distance made me strange.
Wrecked the phone.
Now, I'm alone.
Burn Burn Burn.
Us will never return.

When I looked up, enormous snowflakes were falling. Even if I wanted to sleep, I couldn't because of the loud, jubilant voices celebrating outside. I raced outside to explore. A bunch of people were building snowmen, as well as snow women and nonbinary. Yeah, North South was progressive— or maybe they were afraid of a lawsuit. Ultimately, every snow creature looked indistinguishable. If I had a phone, I would've texted Dorian photos.

In the morning, the snow had stopped, but North South was completely white and eerily silent. The creations from the previous night were completely covered. It was a snow day, well, kind of; all classes were remote. And of course, there was plenty of reading to do. I got some coffee and oatmeal from the cafeteria and got into it. When I got a knock on my door, I figured it was Wally.

"Yo!" I answered.

When Mr. Wells poked his head around my door, I sat up at attention.

"I didn't know it was you."

"Your parents called this morning."

"What's wrong?"

"Nothing, but they're nervous. They want to know that you're okay."

"We're very nervous people. I inherited that gene."

Mr. Wells didn't laugh.

"They want to know that you're okay," Mr. Wells said, concerned. "Please call them. I got to run. Snow is fun for everyone except for the person in charge."

My parents could've emailed me directly, but I figured they wanted an excuse to nudge Mr. Wells. After Mr. Wells left, I trudged over to a pay phone in the cafeteria, one of the few on campus. My mother answered immediately. When we finished discussing the snow, my mother smacked me.

"I know," she said cryptically.

"You know what?" I asked, hiding my displeasure.

"About you and Rosemary."

My heart sped up. I didn't like my mother fishing around. "You're not together."

I took a deep breath and ordered myself to not lose it.

"I know we're not together. I'm at North South, and she's not." If my mother wanted to play cat and mouse, I'd play.

"But you're not a couple," she whined.

You're not a couple. It was jarring to hear aloud, and I didn't want to hear it from anyone, especially my mother.

"Things are strange right now for us," I replied.

Why did I say *us*? There was no us! Why did I say *strange*? I'd vowed to never use that word again.

When I demanded her source, my mother explained that Rosemary had called her because she couldn't reach me on my phone. My mother had grilled it out of her.

"She wanted to make sure you're okay," my mother explained. Great! A mental health checkup call from Rosemary to my parents. I wish Rosemary would stop playing the parents card. You had me. You had my parents. You had it all, until you abandoned us! I was devastated, but I had to feign strength. Anything else and things would deteriorate in a major way.

"Everything'll work out," I said, quoting Dorian's father, Mr. Randolph.

It was my heartbreak, but I was consoling my mother. Soon, I'd do the same for my father.

At least Rosemary hadn't mentioned that she was with someone else. Against all odds, my mother and I were going to end a terrible conversation relatively pleasantly.

"Did you meet Neil?" my mother blurted.

Small miracle: I didn't puke on the spot. By the way she said it, I knew exactly who she was referring to. How did my mother know his name? I didn't know his name. I was exposed. My mother knew everything.

"No, I haven't."

"Well, you're taking this very well. You're quite mature."

"I'm not mature. We both know that. I'm in thirteenth grade!" I wanted to reply.

"Your father and I haven't taken this so well."

"These things happen," I replied in consoling mode. "Try not to think about it."

But we would. We would. We would.

If the *Happy Divorce* student filmmaker heard this conversation, he'd be salivating. When Dylan Mills got dumped, Dylan didn't handle it all too well, but his parents went insane. I changed the subject. There was nothing that either of us could say that would make Rosemary return to us. Instead, we pretended. I asked about Castleton Middle School, Luncheonette, and the weather. As always, they were the same. I promised to email regularly and to call in a few days. After I hung up, I called my father and got a monster reprieve: voice mail.

In the late afternoon, it seemed like everyone was out on the hill just beyond North South Lake. We slid down the hill on plastic slides directly onto the ice. Sherbert and his ridiculously long raccoon hat were the fastest. I almost didn't recognize Quarters in his bright orange North South winter gear. He wasn't sliding.

"I'm retired," he explained. However, he said he was going to give a quick snow angel seminar. Meanwhile, a few vert discers were skating on the lake, tossing a frisbee. When it got dark, everyone packed it in except for a few Society people and their trucks, which had special tires for driving on ice. A few of us stood on the shore and watched them race one another on the frozen lake.

"You want to take a spin out there?" asked Wally.

"Yes, that's exactly what I want to do."

We smiled because we knew that was the last thing I wanted to do.

As I stood on the side of the lake, I had a lingering thought: If these lunatics could race trucks on ice, I could at least get my learner's permit. It was time.

*

North South was no longer postcard perfect. We got a warm spell, and a few days after that, it rained for two days straight. Just as I was getting into some Hammer reading, Wally checked in. When he mentioned that Society had decided to initiate new members, I perked up. No, I didn't want to be a Society member, but I wanted to be asked.

Wally didn't ask.

Confession: I missed being part of something. In the old era, I worked at Luncheonette. I used to be in glee club. I used to be part of the hockey team—barely.

And, of course, I used to be part of us.

A few nights later, North Pole hosted an open mic comedy night. Sherbert was one of the performers, and I wasn't going to miss him. Sherbert's material was unremarkable, but he had this incredible deadpan delivery. Sherbert told the beginning of a joke before abruptly stopping. It was unclear if he was pausing for dramatic effect, or if he forgot the punch line—or both. Was he stoned? Yeah, because Sherbert was always stoned. A Sherbert sample:

Quick, what did the sun say to the clouds?
Hey man! Get out of the way!
What did the camel say to the zebra?
I'll trade you my humps for your stripes.
I never gain weight. Never.
I just get larger clothing.

It was hilarious. Well, maybe you had to be there. You definitely had to be there. I took in the show from one of the
lounge's ultra-comfortable couches. Unfortunately, everyone
besides Sherbert was atrocious, and I shut down . . . until
I emerged in the distance. I was on a motorcycle, wearing
shades and a leather jacket, which had Society's logo on the
front and my last name on the back in big capital letters. I
was owning that machine, riding toward Rosemary . . .

When the lights in the lounge came on, Sherbert was
staring down at me as I opened my eyes, genuinely offended.

"Hey man," Sherbert lisped. "How could you sleep
through my set?"

A few days later, I finally did something I'd been going back
and forth on doing: I asked Wally if I could be in Society.

"Duuude, are you sure you want to do this?" he asked.

"I'm not sure about anything, but I need something."

"Well, this will probably be a first for Society. They probably never had a Barry superfan."

"I wouldn't say I'm exactly a superfan."

"You're a superfan all right. I'll take care of it. No worries."

I was worried that Society wouldn't say yes. And I was
worried if they did say yes.

As usual, Wally did what he said he was going to do. I was
in, and it was happening—soon. Too soon. The initiation
was going down the following Friday. I was told to be in
my room at 5:00, to be prepared to be without a phone,

obviously not a problem, and to have my driver's license, obviously a problem. Fortunately, I was allowed to bring my passport. Yeah, I was joining a motorcycle club, but I didn't even have a driver's license. I asked Wally what to expect, and he just grinned.

"If I told you, it would be no fun," Wally added. Wally took this stuff seriously.

Sure, Wally had my back, but I was anxious. I knew how insane Society could be. I'd been to Society's basement after-hours. I'd seen them race trucks on ice at night. I didn't want to imagine what they'd do to their initiates. I didn't want to eat a bull's scrotum. What did that even taste like? What had I gotten myself into? Well, I asked for it.

I prayed that it wouldn't, but it did: Friday arrived. After classes, I got some lunch and returned to my closet. It was still early. I stared at the door, waiting. I tried to read, but I kept looking at the clock on my laptop. Four o'clock came and went; so did 5:00. I was relieved.

It was over.

Somehow, Society knew that I wasn't feeling it, and they'd bailed on me before I could.

I was out.

They didn't want a tighty-whies-wearing Barry superfan after all. It was for the best. I was destined for predictability, which I was perfectly fine with because I wouldn't have to eat bull's scrotum. I could listen to Barry in peace. No judgements. One happy kid, I dove into some rock reading.

A little after 6:00, a note was slipped under my door.

I was unhappy, again.

    DOWNSTAIRS PARKING LOT
    FIVE MINUTES WITH LAUNDRY BAG &
    DRIVER'S LICENSE

I didn't want to be, but I was in the game. Reluctantly I grabbed my lavender laundry bag—yes mom loves matching—and ran downstairs, where a jacked-up truck was waiting. Someone with an intimidating goatee was in the passenger's seat.

"Get in!" he sternly ordered. "Do you have your driver's license?"

"I have my passport. I was given special permission." Yeah, I sounded like a dweeb. It wasn't like it was the first time.

"Why don't you have your driver's license?"

"I don't drive."

"Pathetic!"

It was.

They drove to a desolate corner and blindfolded me, and we drove around for a while in an unnerving silence. I wanted to hide under my lavender comforter.

We finally stopped. I didn't have a clue of where we were. After more waiting, I was escorted inside a building and ordered to sit. Not too long after, someone ordered, "Take off your blindfolds!"

We were in Society's front room. There were four other guys whom I'd never seen before with laundry bags, and we were surrounded by about two dozen Society members, all of whom had serious expressions. No one was offering spiked cider. One of the female members took out some black and red face paint and started covering our faces with it: half black, half red. I felt a little better. I could handle face paint. After we were painted, the other initiates and I were ordered to form a single-file line and walk outside into a waiting van. None of us spoke a word, but a Society member shouted "Shut up!" Somehow, I controlled my nervous laughter. Yeah, the whole thing seemed ridiculous. In silence, we drove off the North South campus. I was prepared to leave the state.

Actually, I was prepared to leave the country. Yeah, I had my passport.

We drove around North South Lake and stopped at Rich & Dumb's football field, where a game was being played under the stadium lights. We parked behind the bleachers, near the end zone. At least a few thousand people were in attendance. I expected us to be ordered to act like clowns at the game and for everyone to get a laugh at our expense. I could do that, no problem.

But we didn't enter the stadium.

Instead, we sat silently in the van, listening to the dull roar of the R&D crowd. What's next? I didn't dare ask. Just go with it. With fewer than two minutes left in the first half, next arrived.

"Take off your clothes and put 'em in your laundry bag!" ordered a Society member who went by the name Salamander. He was tall, lean, and very pale, with longish strawberry blond hair.

"You're joking, right?" the largest of the initiates blurted out. My thoughts exactly.

"Shut up and strip! Put your clothes and anything else in your laundry bag!" Salamander ordered. "They're not going anywhere. We'll hold them for you."

"Will my passport be safe?" I quietly asked.

"What, Nut Hugger?" yelled Salamander.

I hated my new nickname.

"You shouldn't knock 'em before you try them," I thought to myself. "I have a question," I barely muttered.

"Does that include our underwear?"

"Yeah, take off those nut huggers, Nut Hugger!" Salamander ordered, as he chuckled at himself.

We were streaking at halftime. Salamander told us it would be a blast. Yeah, right, blast! I should've known that we'd be streaking. What was with Society and getting naked? It was one thing to strip down to your tighty-whities in a dark, wet basement in the middle of the night. It was something else completely to get completely naked in public at R&D. I wanted out, but I did not move, and I did not remove an article of clothing. Meanwhile, the other initiates were already naked, their clothing deposited in their laundry bags.

"If you don't want to do this, that's fine. You can bail, Nut Hugger. When I saw your purple laundry bag, I figured you were a question mark."

"It's lavender," I blurted.

"What was that?" barked Salamander.

"My laundry bag is lavender."

"Are you in or are you out?"

As much as I wanted to be out, I was in. I had to be. Wally had vouched for me. And as much as I hate to admit it, I wanted, no, I needed to show Rosemary I was a different person. I wasn't just a pathetic, glee club dropout, fifth-string goalie. I wasn't just waiting for her texts.

I could be part of something other than us.

As I disrobed, I started singing to myself. It kept my mind off what we were about to do. It helped me deal.

You were someone I wanted to impress, so I got undressed.

When I was completely naked, nut huggers, socks, and everything, I sat nervously with my hands over my privates and repeated the words in my head. I looked like an awkward, orange giraffe. Salamander showed us a map of the stadium, but I barely glanced at it. I was way too self-conscious.

I heard the gist of it. We were to run the length of the football field, through the opposite end zone, and into the adjacent trees. After about 150 yards in the trees, we'd bump into Lakeside Road, where transportation would be waiting.

"When the last player hits the tunnel at halftime, we're running!" Salamander ordered.

We? You're not running anywhere.

When the half was seconds from ending, Salamander drove us to the end zone behind the goalposts where there were no fans and a mere security rope. We watched the players exit the field.

"When I open the door, run the fastest you've ever run in your life!" Salamander ordered.

"What about security?" I mumbled.

"What Nut Hugger?" Salamander snarled.

"Nothing."

"Good. It's time. Have fun boys!" Salamander ordered as he slid open the van door.

"Now, go!"

I was the last to file out. It was on, and I was sprinting as if I were being chased by pack of man-eating wolverines. I was juiced, too juiced. If I hadn't ducked at the last second, I would've run directly into the security rope.

It was a relatively warm evening, but there had been a slight drizzle earlier, and the turf was slick. Within seconds, I was approaching midfield. No, this wasn't so bad. Actually, it was an enormous adrenaline rush. It was liberating. I was single and free. If this was living, I was living!

Surprisingly, there seemed to be no crowd reaction. They didn't care, or maybe they were confused. I was confused. What was the point? And then I was on the forty, the thirty-five. I turned to the crowd for a quick moment. Some people seemed to be smiling and yelling. Others looked stunned, or perhaps they were embarrassed that they were witnessing such a spectacle. They were snobs at R&D. As I got closer to the end zone, I felt victorious. Memo to the universe: Dylan Mills isn't predictable. I raised both my hands in victory!

I'd won.

And then I lost. My balance. I desperately tried to stay upright—stumbling for what seemed like ten yards—but gravity won out, and I wound up flopping face-first, not quite landing in the end zone. Finally, the crowd released a roar, much louder than anything I'd heard during the actual game. When I finally rose to my feet and looked up, I was alone. My fellow initiates were gone, already in the woods, close to the getaway cars. Fear quickly replaced any adrenaline. I was horrified to see four or five security men and women in neon yellow shirts lumbering toward me. I wasn't liberated anymore. I was just a stupid naked freckled North Stoner. Surrender immediately was the wise move, but I panicked and started running toward the opposite end zone. The security people were no match. It wasn't because I was that fast. They were that slow. Now the crowd was completely into it. I'd run through the opposite end zone, under the lame security rope and back to North South. It was less than two miles. Easy. As I was approaching the end zone, another herd of security people suddenly appeared.

Where did all this security come from?

I made the smart choice, finally. Just as I stopped and raised my hands in surrender, everything became nothing.

*

When I opened my eyes, I was in a hospital gown in the emergency room. I felt fine, but I felt something strange on my face. When I got in front of a mirror, I was horrified. My face and hands were covered with paint.

I needed that time machine again. No, it wasn't a bad dream.

A nice nurse informed me that I lost consciousness after one of the R&D security women tackled me. As a precaution, I was taken to the hospital. I must've showered for at least fifteen minutes.

When Mr. Wells entered my curtained-off space, I couldn't look at him, much less talk to him. I was so embarrassed. As Mr. Wells tersely informed me that R&D wasn't pressing charges, I pretended to be drowsy. Other than that though, Mr. Wells said nothing. After I was cleared to leave, I quickly dressed, and we left in Mr. Wells's truck.

"I'm going to have to suspend you for a week," Mr. Wells said calmly but sternly, looking directly at the road. "I've already notified your professors."

"I didn't want to do it. I apologize."

I bowed my head as tears slowly rolled down my face. I'd failed the initiation. I'd proved nothing to Rosemary. And I was suspended. I was a disaster.

"Apology accepted," Mr. Wells replied in a low voice, still not looking at me. "I get it. It's a joke, and I like a joke as much as the next guy, but—" his voice simmered with emotion.

"North South is not a joke. I want North South to be taken seriously. We deserve to be taken seriously. We're building something special here. We're North South. We're *not* North Stoned!"

Mr. Wells's words were jarring. I'd done it. I'd hurt Mr. Wells. I'd hurt North South. I was so ashamed. A suspension was getting off easy. Mr. Wells should have made me walk back to the North Pole. I deserved to be expelled.

"As always, my door is open if you want to talk," Mr. Wells offered as he dropped me off.

I quickly apologized again and ran off to my closet, praying that no one would see me. No one did.

I was alone.

I barely slept. Instead, I forced myself to do school-work, as if that would somehow undo the damage. At dawn, I walked uptown. I couldn't face anyone. I needed comfort.

Pancakes.

Pancakes would cure me, at least for a few hours. I'd get pancakes and then hide in one of the private rooms in the library and study.

Just as I was walking across the street, I spotted the bus in the distance, the one I took to campus. It was southbound. I boarded, paid the driver cash and took a seat. Why not? I was suspended for a week. Nothing was keeping me here. And now more than ever, I needed Luncheonette's pumpkin cinnamon pancakes.

When I reached Castleton, the first thing I did was get a phone. I needed to talk to someone other than myself. I left messages for each of my parents and Dorian. Instantly, she called back.

"Is that *you*?" Dorian shouted.

"Yeah, it's me. I got a new phone. Why are you screaming?"

"I mean is that you on the internet?"

Is that you on the internet? A question you never want to face in your lifetime. Trust me.

"What are you talking about?"

"I'd recognize those freckles anywhere. You're streaking on that football field. It's hilarious."

Pumpkin cinnamon pancakes were now out of the question. I was ill.

"How'd you see it?"

"It's everywhere. You haven't seen it?"

"No!"

"You should."

"No, I shouldn't. I don't need to see myself naked. If anyone asks, I'm denying it's me."

"Those freckles are undeniable," Dorian laughed.

"This isn't funny."

"I know. But it is, a little. We'll laugh at this when we're ninety!"

"Yes, let's please wait seventy-two years to laugh," I snapped.

Dorian was laughing so hard she could barely speak.

"You're very funny, Dylan Mills."

"I'll trade you some funny for some smarts."

Dorian laughed again. "You're plenty smart."

"I'm so smart I got suspended for a week."

"It was worth it. It was hilarious. But why'd you do it?"

"It was for North South's motorcycle club."

"Motorcycle club? When did *you* get into motorcycles?"

"I didn't. You know me. I'm strictly bicycle material."

"Yeah, a motorcycle club doesn't sound like you."

"I know, but that's exactly why I did it."

*

When I got home, I was befuddled. My mother was out, but my father's car was in the driveway. They had memberships at the same indoor tennis facility, and they were probably playing. It was a worthwhile investment, better than therapy, at least for my parents. They could take out their aggression on a yellow ball. Mr. Wells had already notified them about my suspension.

I flipped on the television, but I got what I expected: The same movies that I'd seen a zillion times already were on. After I distracted myself with some reading, I called Wally, but he didn't answer. Unlike the rest of the world, he wasn't connected to his phone. I left a quick voice mail.

When my parents entered the living room each holding their tennis racquets, we didn't utter a word—but we embraced for a long moment. It was our first group hug—ever. After we were hugged out, we sat down in the living room, and I braced myself for an interrogation. This time, I had it coming.

"Were you kicked off campus too?" asked my father.

"No, I just needed a time-out," I said solemnly.

"Why did you do this, Dylan?" asked my mother.

"It wasn't my idea. It was a prank. It's a long story, but I was trying to be someone I wasn't."

"Was this about Rosemary?" my father asked.

"What isn't?"

My parents nodded. They understood. They would've run naked through a football stadium for Rosemary too.

"What's funny about you running naked at a football stadium?" asked my father. "I'm not laughing."

"I don't know."

"You have to have a lot of confidence to run naked in front of a full stadium," my mother said.

"Well, it wasn't full. It was at least half empty," I added.

"Maybe we can ask for the suspension to be cut in half," quipped my father. He tapped my mother's shoulder for emphasis.

"Jacob, you're the funny one," my mother laughed.

What was going on?

My parents weren't upset, and they seemed gleeful.

"Well, of course, we're not pleased that you're suspended, but we're very happy you're home," said my mother. "We've got some yard work for you to do, and we have a lot to discuss."

My parents nodded in agreement at one another. And suddenly, everything turned serious and even weirder. My mother rested her hand on my father's knee.

After some unnerving silence, I finally asked pointedly, "What is going on?"

"I'm living here," my father explained.

"Great!" I replied. "Did Mom move into your studio?"

"I'm living here too, silly," laughed my mother.

"You're living together?"

"Yes!" they said in unison as they clasped hands.

"But aren't you divorced? This isn't how normal people—"

"We're engaged!"

"Engaged for *what*?"

I knew, but I didn't want to know.

"Marriage, of course," said my mother.

"But you were already married, and you're happily divorced. You told me that you've never been happier. My entire school believes that you're the happiest divorced couple on the planet."

"We needed a time-out too," my mother explained. "We've reconciled."

"But we all agreed that you were miserable together. We *were* miserable."

"Yes," my father said slowly. "But it's all relative. We were much more miserable apart. We're much less miserable together."

At that moment, I had a revelation: Our single solitary goal for our entire lives was less misery.

"It's the lesser of two evils," my mother added.

As I watched them look into one another's eyes, their arms wrapped around one another, I was stunned silent. I don't recall ever witnessing such affection in my lifetime.

And I didn't want to witness it now, but I played along.

We celebrated by ordering in Thai, which Castleton did very well, and North South didn't do. There were no toasts, but there was also no arguing or "lively debate," as my father referred to it. And for the first time in I don't know how long, my parents didn't mention Rosemary. For so long, she'd been everything. Now I was suspended and single, but my parents had found forever. When I hit the pillow, I felt a glimmer of hope. I slept well until I was awakened by a text.

Dorian.

> Rosemary is trying to get in touch with you. Can I give her your new number?

I texted back:

I'll get back to you about Rosemary. My parents are remarrying. More later.

Rosemary.

For weeks, I'd take anything she'd throw my way. Now I didn't want it. Well, I wanted it but not on these terms. Rosemary contacted me out of curiosity, or worse she called concerning my safety. It was as if I were a charity case. Any hope I had from the night before was gone. I tried to force myself back to sleep but couldn't.

Just a day earlier, I had my heart set on Luncheonette's pumpkin cinnamon pancakes and seeing the Luncheonette family. Now I wanted no such thing. I figured that they'd all seen my streaking video. Besides that, a visit to Luncheonette would remind me of my last brunch with Rosemary. If I returned alone, everyone would ask about her, or why I wasn't with her. I'm sure everyone had already heard that we weren't together, but the usual suspects would want to hear it directly from me.

"I always knew she was too good for him," I imagined Mr. Z whispering to a nodding Mrs. Z. I hadn't heard Mr. Z's voice in a while, but now he was back.

It was best to stay clear of Luncheonette for now.

My parents gave me plenty of chores, including dismantling our backyard wooden spaceship. Dismantling and disposing it wasn't too difficult, but it was more emotional than I imagined. Yeah, my eyes even got a little wet. It was more official than ever.

No one was going to Mars.

I never wanted to hear that song again. It was a new era, yeah, another one. As I arranged the wood from my dismantled spaceship, I came to another decision.

For dinner, my father made a wonderful pasta dish with seafood. Before the divorce, his culinary skills were nonexistent. A happy divorce had its good points.

"When are you returning to school?" my father asked.

"I was planning on staying here for the entire week."

Lie.

I wasn't ready to tell anyone my decision. I wasn't returning to North South. I wanted a fresh start—immediately. I'd completed almost all of the semester work; I received very good grades, the best grades of my, uh, uneven academic career; and I had an excellent rapport with my professors. Besides tarnishing North South's already fragile reputation with my indecent exposure, I was an exemplary student. I'd finish the semester remotely. I was confident that my other professors would go for it. I'd already left a voice mail for Berkowitz. If my professors didn't go for my plan, it'd be just another incomplete for Dylan Mills. It wouldn't be like it was the first time.

*

Before I stepped into Luncheonette, I braced myself for a deluge of questions and whispers. But no one seemed to have a clue about the video.

Memo to Dylan Mills: It's not all about you.

People want to eat! Good news: Mr. Nillson informed me that I had a position at Luncheonette whenever I needed it. Of course for my new plan to work, I needed it. I'd figure the rest out, eventually, maybe.

Sunday arrived. I'd been at home for a week, and I still hadn't gotten around to telling my parents that I wasn't returning to North South. Maybe I wouldn't. I just wouldn't go back, and they'd figure it out. Their heads were in the clouds anyway with their marriage do-over. As I lay on my bed procrastinating, my mother knocked on the door.

"Dylan, honey," my mother said. My mother hadn't called me *honey* in forever. What was going on? "We have a surprise for you."

"Please, no surprises!" I pleaded.

Any mention of surprise triggered something.

"I understand," growled a familiar gravelly voice.

Berkowitz!

"I wouldn't want to see me either!"

They laughed.

I panicked.

It was happening. Berkowitz was in my house, outside my room. I'd heard about Berkowitz showing up at his students' dorms or even homes, but I'd always assumed it was some kind of North South myth. But should I really be surprised? Berkowitz had volunteered for solitary confinement. After everything that had happened, I wasn't ready to face him. I didn't know if I'd ever be.

"How long are you going to have me wait out here?" Berkowitz bellowed as I considered my options.

I had none.

I exhaled and slowly opened the door. Berkowitz was more formal than usual. He had on a blazer, a crisp white shirt, and a tie in North South's colors. His wild curly hair was brushed down, almost tame. It was Berkowitz, Castleton style, and it worked. Berkowitz scanned my room as my mother stood in my doorway. I gave her a look, and she took the hint. She'd gotten better. I guess we all had. Berkowitz eyed the only chair in my room.

"May I?" he asked. I nodded. Berkowitz sat down and smiled. Berkowitz laughed a lot, but he didn't smile all too often, if ever.

"I'm sorry about what happened," I said. Right after I said it, I knew what was coming.

"Don't be sorry. Make it better! And what do you have to be sorry about anyway?"

"Streaking, embarrassing North South . . ."

"Embarrass North South? You made us proud. You put on an incredible show. I've never laughed so hard. Never!"

"You saw it?"

"Who hasn't?"

"My parents."

"Well, they don't need to see it."

"I got suspended. I made a fool of myself!"

"You played a fool for one night!" shouted Berkowitz. "Who cares about football? You made a meaningless game meaningful and fun. You put R&D football on the map! You made things better!"

"Really?"

"Yes, really. I wouldn't lie!"

When we were done laughing, I told Berkowitz about everything that had transpired with Rosemary over the course of the semester. I didn't shed any tears, but Berkowitz did. I handed him a tissue. When I was done, neither of us said anything for a while. I had nothing left, but Berkowitz had plenty.

"I had a great love once," Berkowitz began.

I didn't want to hear about Berkowitz's first love. It was just too weird—but there was no escape.

"She was a fellow professor, political science, which I absolutely detest. I hate everything to do with politics. If you want to talk about lying, don't get me started. . . . But this woman understood me."

"What happened?"

"I didn't understand her!" Berkowitz shouted. "By the time I figured things out, she had tenure at another school."

"Did you follow her?"

"Eventually, but I was too late. She was with someone else."

"And then what?"

"I was absolutely devastated. Devastated! It was the worst time in my life. I shut down. I felt sorry for myself. I didn't make anything better! Do you know what happened?"

How would I know what happened?

"No."

"I got older. And I threw myself into my work. I spent three months in solitary confinement and wrote *Alone*. It was a gruesome, gruesome time but my most productive."

"Do you still think about her?"

"Every day. . . . As much as I tried, life doesn't stop for no one. No one! We must go on because life goes on." We sat for a few moments in silence, absorbing it all.

"Do you know why I teach?" Berkowitz asked rhetorically. "I teach because of my students. You make me better. I want to hear your ideas. They're fresh, most of the time. It keeps me on my toes. It keeps me spry. Well, I'm not quite spry, but I aspire to be. . . . If you have your heart set on chasing Rosemary, you should. Who am I to stand in the way? I'm just an old sociology professor. Who is anyone to stand in your way. But—"

And here was the "but."

"But now, now we need to finish what we started, and that is our first semester at North South. We started strong. Let's finish stronger. After that, we'll figure out *our* next move. Deal?"

*

After showering, I arrived just in time to hear my mother gushing to Berkowitz, "We're going to the Caribbean over Christmas break for our honeymoon!" It was great that my parents had decided to live a life of less misery. However, I didn't ever want to hear "honeymoon" and "my parents" in the same sentence. All of that was supposed to take place *before* me.

Before driving back to North South, Berkowitz insisted on dining at Luncheonette.

"I've heard so much about it. Now I must see it for myself. I didn't come all this way just to see *you*!" Berkowitz yelled before laughing. I had major reservations about taking Berkowitz to Luncheonette. I just didn't see the pair jelling.

I've been wrong about a lot of things in my relatively short life, and this was just another. When Berkowitz walked through Luncheonette's doors, it was as if he were a regular. Mr. Randolph had read *Alone*, and they instantly connected. And then something happened that never happens at Luncheonette. Much of the restaurant abandoned their feasts to hear Berkowitz, who was flanked by my parents. I stood off in the background. I wanted a good view. I didn't hear all of it, but I probably heard most of it in one form or another before. Mr. and Mrs. Z hung on Berkowitz's every word, enthusiastically nodding along. Mr. Z even asked him where he could get a North South tie. It did look good. At one point, Berkowitz mentioned the importance of education and described my parents as "bedrocks of society," which made my parents beam. I laughed to myself: I had to go to North South to get my parents the recognition they craved and deserved.

After almost an hour, Berkowitz told everyone that we had to be on our way.

"I have an 8:00 a.m. on Monday!" he shouted. "We don't just smoke great dope up there!" Luncheonette howled. Berkowitz shook every hand, and there were a lot, and then he turned to me.

"Let's scram!" he declared. After I embraced my parents, Berkowitz placed his arm around me, and we strode out of Luncheonette's doors.

I'd return to Castleton a winner—finally.

We were a step out the door before Berkowitz did an about-face and ran inside. I don't think he forgot anything. He hadn't brought anything.

"Hey, folks, just one more thing," Berkowitz announced. "Don't complain! Don't criticize! MAKE IT BETTER!"

"Did I get a little carried away in there?" Berkowitz asked when we were on the thruway.

"No, not at all."

He was Berkowitz being himself. If anyone got carried away, it was the Luncheonette crowd. Berkowitz brought something out in them, all positive. Berkowitz was good for Castleton.

"I'm famished." Berkowitz had been so busy holding court he forgot to eat. Fortunately, I'd taken some pumpkin cinnamon pancakes for the ride. Berkowitz pulled over at the next way station and indulged heartily. Luncheonette more than lived up to Berkowitz's expectations.

When we were within striking distance of North South, my phone rang.

Rosemary.

How did she get my number? It didn't matter at this point. She had it.

I wanted to talk to Rosemary. I didn't. I really didn't.

But I did.

Yeah, it was complicated, or maybe it wasn't. Facts were facts: She was with him, not me. She was embarrassed that I went to North South. I wasn't taking the call. I was in a car with Berkowitz. I was going to hide. I was good at that. If North South had a hide-and-seek team, I'd be All-American. I'd get around to talking to Rosemary Silversmith, eventually, maybe.

And then I had a change of heart.

If I had to talk to Rosemary, it would be better with Berkowitz. Berkowitz gave me strength. This man would protect me.

"Hi," I replied casually.

"Hey. Your parents gave me your new number. I—"

"I'm in a car," I interrupted.

"Who's driving?"

Rosemary was asking, but she was also telling me that I *wasn't* driving.

"Berkowitz."

"Berkowitz?" Rosemary asked.

I'd forgotten. She didn't even know about Berkowitz. Rosemary knew nothing about North South—besides that we had awesome weed.

"He's my sociology professor and my adviser." Berkowitz looked over at me, raising an eyebrow.

"And I'm your friend, damn it!" When Berkowitz said that it made my heart swell. He was my friend, a really good friend.

"He sounds funny," Rosemary giggled.

"He's hilarious." Berkowitz shot me a dead serious look. "And he's written a ton of incredible books. I took him to Luncheonette."

"You took him to Luncheonette?" Rosemary asked incredulously.

"Yes, with my parents."

"Really?"

"Yes. It has been quite a day."

"Wow. It's very cool that you're on a road trip with one of your professors."

"Well, it's not really a road trip, but it's cool."

"It feels like a road trip," interjected Berkowitz.

"I never went on the road with one of my professors," Rosemary groaned.

"Well, you've got plenty of time to make it happen."

"Dylan, can I ask you a question?"

"I don't know, can you?" I was stalling. When someone asks you permission to ask a question, how could that question be good?

"Seriously."

"I'd rather not—but okay."

"Why were you streaking on the football field?"

My heart stopped. After Berkowitz showed up at my house, I'd forgotten about my video.

"Yes," I replied before pausing.

"That was hilarious!" Rosemary laughed. "What has gotten into you?"

"I'm trying to get you out of my system, and I'm also still trying to impress you," I would've said if I were being entirely truthful. Yeah, I know. It's complicated. Instead, I replied, "I'm not quite sure."

"Why'd you do it?"

"It's a long story." Translation: I don't want to discuss it now.

"I got a long, long time."

Now, Rosemary had a long, long time.

"I can't be rude to Berkowitz."

"You can be rude to Berkowitz!" Berkowitz snapped.

"Can we talk later?" I asked.

Of course, we could talk later. I was saying goodbye, and Rosemary seemed surprised. At that moment, I had a disturbing revelation: Never in the history of our relationship had I gotten off the phone first. Until now, Rosemary had called the shots. Every shot.

"Sure," Rosemary replied in a noticeably softer voice. "We can talk later."

It was a lie. I didn't want to talk later. I was taking Berkowitz's advice. I was living in the present. No, time doesn't stop for no one.

*

North South was in perfect condition—for polar bears. It was frigid, and several inches of fresh snow was on the ground. I ran through the fluffy stuff in my new heavy-duty boots, a gift from my parents. The Mills family had matching boots. The store had offered a special: Buy two pairs, get the third for 50 percent off. They were just right for North South.

When I rushed into the theater, mere seconds to spare, the entire class was already seated, and Hammer was staring at me.

"You really know how to make an entrance, Mr. Mills," Hammer commented in her weird accent. "You put on quite a show the other night. Wonderful theater! Would you like to say a few words?"

"No, not really," I replied awkwardly.

Everyone laughed.

"Well, you let your performance speak for itself. It was grand. Now, what will you do for an encore? Expectations are very high for your final semester performance."

Yeah, I'd messed up again. I'd procrastinated about my final performance, which accounted for a third of my grade. I'd kept telling myself that I'd get around to planning something, but then I got suspended, and, well, I just didn't. It was in a week, on the final day of classes right before Thanksgiving break, and I didn't have a clue of what I was going to perform.

Now Hammer had *expectations.*

That word still got to me.

Growing up, I'd lowered expectations, so I wouldn't be disappointed. I wound up disappointed because I had such low expectations. I'd say it's funny how that works—but it's not funny.

After class, students stopped me to shake my hand and introduce themselves. Who would think it? Streaking: the great icebreaker.

It was all good, but I still had to come up with a performance. The obvious choice was to sing something, yes, a solo. I was still petrified of singing a solo in public, but I didn't know what else to do. I was considering a Barry song—maybe a heavy metal version. Wally and Jimmy were into that, but I wasn't sure. And too many students had already sung. A girl blew me away with a show tunes medley. A few vert discers did a doo-wop version of the Canadian national anthem. A guy belted out opera as he juggled melting snowballs. He did both horribly, but it was hilarious. As original as heavy metal Barry is, it's still Barry. For my first public solo, my gut told me I needed to do something that was all mine.

I slept on it. I was good at that.

The very next day in the cafeteria, Sherbert stopped me. He'd heard that I was trying to come up with something for my performance, and he wanted to help.

"You're a wonderful sleeper," Sherbert lisped. "You should just take your bed to the stage and pass out."

"And then what?"

"You'll sleep."

"And then?"

"Well, you'll be sleeping, so whatever you do when you sleep. I don't know. You might have a dream. You might snore. You might talk in your sleep. You might walk and talk in your sleep. You might sing in your sleep. That would be a trip. I don't know. We'll see how many hours people stick around to watch you do whatever you do when you sleep!"

"You don't think it will be boring?"

"It's avant-garde performance art!"

Avant-garde performance art can be boring, I thought. But I didn't say anything. Sherbert was trying to help.

"Can I sleep on it?"

"You're a riot, Mills." Sherbert laughed as his eyes lit up.

"But I *really* want to sleep on it."

After four nights of sleeping on it, I woke up with something—something that would require Sherbert's help. It wasn't sleeping on stage. I needed someone who could edit video, and Sherbert could do that, even when he was stoned, which was all the time.

After a couple days, I went to 420 to present what I'd produced with Sherbert's help. Wally, Jimmy, and Sherbert took seats in front of my laptop. I explained that it was just a rough cut—definitely not a final version—and I clicked the file on my computer. My life appeared:

> Home movie footage courtesy of the Mills family: A young me waves in front of the Castleton Community Swimming Pool. I dive into the pool and disappear. My father stands off to the side of the pool with a stopwatch and follows my underwater movements. By his side, my mother shouts enthusiastic encouragement.

> Cut to a watercolor painting of mine: I'm in front of the pool. My hands are raised in victory, and my parents are on each side of me, each holding a hand. We are the champions!

> Cut to a photo of me in my silver space suit: I'm proudly standing with my space camp certificate.

> Cut to home movie footage: We're in our space suits, sitting in our backyard spaceship, giving the thumbs up.

> Cut to a watercolor painting of mine: Our backyard spaceship blasts off from our yard.

> Cut to home movie footage: I'm playing Barry at a piano recital. Audience applause.

Blank screen

Cut to newsreel footage: My parents and I are in front of our house, and a reporter is interviewing us.

REPORTER: "We're here with the Mills family. They'll be traveling to North Carolina to compete in the National Hollering Championships. They've been practicing for months, and they think they can win it all."

DANA MILLS: "Even when we're quiet, people think we're noisy. I prefer to describe us as enthusiastic. I think it's genetic. Some people think we're cursed. We think we're blessed."

We holler Barry at the championships.

Cut to a watercolor painting of mine: We stand proudly with our fourth-place ribbon.

Cut to newsreel footage:

DANA MILLS: "We'll be back next year. We're not going to stop hollering anytime soon. We can't stop. It's in our DNA!"

Credits roll: Director: Dylan Mills; Editor: Sherbert; Watercolor: Dylan Mills

When my computer screen cut to black, there was silence. They were speechless because they were impressed, hopefully. Or maybe they were horrified.

"What do you think?" I asked tentatively. "It's not the final version, and I know it needs narration."

"It's funny," said Wally. "But it'd be funnier if you added the streaking video."

"That would be awesome!" lisped Sherbert.

"No one wants to see me naked," I snapped.

"Duuude, everyone wants to see you naked," said Wally. "You have over 800,000 views!"

"Great, thanks for the update," I replied, turning to Jimmy. "What do you think?"

"It's good enough," said Jimmy flatly.

Jimmy's review hit me hard: I didn't want to be just good enough, not anymore.

"How can I improve it?"

"It's already memorable, but if you want it to be unforgettable, it needs something, something to pull it together. It needs your voice."

"Well, I was planning on narrating it."

"Yeah," said Jimmy in a drawn-out skeptical way that was really saying, "No!"

"I want you to think about this long and hard: What can Dylan Mills bring to this that no one else can?"

*

It was standing room only. A lot of students who weren't in Hammer's class showed up too, including a few from Rich & Dumb. Altogether, a good three hundred were in North South's theater to check out my final performance. I can thank Wally for the enormous turnout. He'd dropped a rumor that I was going to reenact my R&D streak. Nudity: It's supposedly the most natural thing, but people treat it like it's the weirdest. Regardless, Hammer was thrilled. Wearing a burgundy scarf that touched her knees, she took center stage and enthusiastically announced us in her signature accent: "Ladies and gentlemen, please welcome Party Animal!" Wally dimmed the theater lights. Jimmy strummed his acoustic, staying in the shadows. Yes, he was wearing his shades, as well as a black bolero hat, which would work only for him. I nervously approached the mic at the center of the stage, took a deep breath, and let it out.

I'm swimming underwater, but I never won a race.

I was doing it, finally, singing a solo—in public. Well, I wasn't completely solo. Sherbert had pressed play, and our video was playing on the stage's large screen.

> *We're bracing for takeoff, but we're blasting off to nowhere.*
> *Yelling notes here, brushing colors there.*
> *We'll take it as far as we can go.*
> *But what if we're so-so?*
> *Yo!*
> *Sometimes when you fail, you win.*
> *Not trying is the sin.*

When the screen went black, Jimmy exchanged his acoustic for his electric. A moment after my streaking footage hit the screen, the audience went bonkers.

> *There was someone I wanted to impress.*
> *So I got undressed.*
> *It wasn't my style.*
> *But it went viral.*

My privates were covered by a large black circle, which provoked even more hysteria. The three hundred sounded like three thousand. Never did I think that my tall, freckled frame would evoke such joy. Yeah, Wally was right. With the audience on its feet, I kept going.

> *I'm not a party animal.*
> *But I can still party.*
> *I tried to be some other kind of thing.*
> *But all I needed was to sing.*
> *I'm not a party animal.*
> *But I can still party!!*
> *Yeah!*

After we hit our last note, the audience applauded and didn't stop. They remained standing. Quarters had a prime center seat in the audience. I think I saw Berkowitz somewhere in the back, well at least his hair, which was back to its unruly self. We dragged Sherbert up to the stage to take a bow with us. He was bashful, and both of us had to pull him on stage. Hammer insisted that we take questions from the audience.

"Where'd you get the actors?" someone asked.

"They're not actors," Jimmy scolded. "That's real footage of Dylan and his parents."

"How are your folks?" another student yelled out. "They're super cool!"

"They're getting hitched again," I answered.

"Well, that's wonderful!" Hammer added. "Bravo!"

"How'd Sherbert get involved?" someone yelled.

"We'll let Sherbert take that one," I replied.

Jimmy, Wally, and I nodded at Sherbert, encouraging him to speak.

"Well, I don't know," Sherbert began, lispin' more than usual in a low voice. He was obviously nervous.

"You gotta speak up," someone from the audience yelled. "We can't hear you."

We handed Sherbert the mic.

"Well, I got wicked stoned one day and put Dylan's bed on the basketball court. I thought it was funny, at least at the time. Anyway, I promised to make it up to Dylan so Wally wouldn't kick my ass. I guess that's how I initially got involved, and it went from there."

"Sherbert—is that your name?" Hammer asked as if is she was referring to an exotic delicacy.

"That's what people call me, so I guess so," Sherbert replied.

Everyone laughed.

"Listen up folks, in all seriousness, there's a lesson to be learned from this," Hammer said in a serious tone. "Creativity can have the most unorthodox beginnings. You must be open to anything, anyone, and everything."

"Why'd you tell *this* story?" someone asked.

"Well it's my story. I figured it's the one I should tell before I tell someone else's. I'm a beginner."

"Don't sell yourself short, Mr. Mills," Hammer said, pointing her finger at me for emphasis.

When there were no more questions, everyone applauded once more, and Hammer wished everyone a happy Thanksgiving before dismissing us.

An hour later, I was on my way back to Castleton once again—but not on a bus. A North South kid who lived close to Castleton offered to give me a ride home. He wanted to travel with the cool streaker. Never saw that coming.

*

It was the holidays, and Luncheonette was more insane than usual. Most would probably consider it a drag to work over Thanksgiving break. I didn't. I was grateful. It was nice to be needed, the pay was at least double, and it put some distance between me and my parents' frequent acts of affection.

It also kept my mind off Rosemary, well, most of the time. It was a work in progress, but I was making progress.

Thanksgiving Eve was different from others though. Luncheonette was consumed with The Taliban Kid, who was embroiled in some sort of controversy. The night before, Dorian had filled me in on the main details. A few days earlier, a popular college blogger, Joe College, known as JC, alleged that TTK—who had racked up half a million Instagram followers—was not who he said he was. According to JC, TTK was born and bred in a comfortable town just forty-five minutes west of Castleton, not too far from Rosemary's lake house. His parents, as well as his grandparents, were alive and well in this same town. They had no Taliban affiliation.

Yeah, according to JC, TTK was a fraud.

TTK denied the allegations, but JC produced photos from TTK's elementary school. In one, he was wearing a spelling bee ribbon. In another, he was playing baseball. TTK claimed the photos were photoshopped. I figured that the story would end there, but it didn't. Other bloggers and news outlets started weighing in. It all seemed preposterous. Someone was waging a campaign against TTK because they were jealous. Typical Castleton. Anyway, as Luncheonette indulged, more than a few diners kept an eye on TTK's Instagram, awaiting his next denial. I expected TTK to provide proof of his background. I didn't quite know how he'd do it. It's not like the Taliban gives certificates, right?

At noon, TTK finally spoke.

I was hustling at Luncheonette, but I got the highlights. It was all a lie. The Taliban Kid wasn't The Taliban Kid. He *was* Jake Simmons. Jake claimed that it was a joke that spiraled out of control. TTK shed a few tears and asked for forgiveness and for everyone to believe he was sincere in his mission of "peace, love, and everything in between." He promised to donate 20 percent of his profits from his acorn necklaces and energy plants to wounded veterans everywhere, not just in his "native United States."

"I can't believe it," I muttered to Dorian's father, Mr. Randolph.

"TTK's a great actor," Mr. Randolph laughed. "But he's an even better businessman. I still can't believe that he gets people to pay $50 for those ridiculous acorns."

Others were much less forgiving. Mr. and Mrs. Z were livid.

"He should be locked up in Guantanamo!" Mr. Z repeatedly railed.

On the way back to North South—no, not on the bus— I checked TTK's Instagram. I expected it to be down, but it wasn't. And business was excellent. Since his admission, TTK had doubled his number of followers, and I saw that he was doing paid public speaking engagements. Dorian heard TTK, uh, Jake was getting $5,000 a pop.

DECEMBER

I didn't set foot in the North South library. Whenever I was conscious, I was in my closet studying. I'd taken Berkowitz's words to heart. I wanted to finish strong. I would finish strong.

When I started at North South, my main source of academic agita was geology. Four months in, nothing had changed, but I was better at dealing with it, yeah, thanks to Wally's masterful tutoring. Berkowitz said he despised exams, but he gave one, an open book, straight shot of seventy-five multiple-choice questions "to placate the powers that be."

After North South's final final, the entire campus went uptown. North South shut down its main street, so everyone could congregate in the street and celebrate.

"Nice shorts," complimented Sam, who'd snuck up behind me. I was wearing a funky pair of North South board shorts. We'd had a string of unseasonably warm days, so we weren't bundled up like we were at the real North Pole.

"Thanks!" I replied. I'd been to a few of Sam's scrimmages and games, and we'd seen each other around on the way to class, but we hadn't spoken much at all. Yeah, I still felt awkward around her. But in this euphoric North Southed moment, most of that was gone.

"We made it!" Sam yelled.

"It still hasn't hit me yet. I feel like I should be memorizing minerals."

"Yeah, I know. I know. Thanks for supporting the team. It means so much. We appreciate it. I appreciate it."

"Well, you guys are awesome."

"Well, I don't know about that. We're 0−2."

"But you won some scrimmages."

"We won a scrimmage."

"Well, you've been in every game."

"And you really killed your theater performance." Sam smiled. "'I'm not a party animal, but I can still party!' Love that."

Yeah, it sounded much, much better when she said it.

"You were there?"

"Of course. Who wasn't? And we support each other. That's what friends do. And I heard you were running through the theater naked or something." Sam laughed.

"It's good to hear you say that."

"What? That I wanted to see you naked?"

I blushed.

"Well that's nice . . . but I was referring to the friends thing. I consider you a friend too."

"Well we're friends. Great. It took us a while to figure that out. Cool. We got a few games over break. What are you up to?"

"I'll be back home, working. The money's good, and it's fun, well, sometimes. They're talking about promoting me to server."

"Nice!" Sam high-fived me. "And you'll get some quality time with the lady."

"No, there'll be none of that," I shrugged. "That crashed and burned. I'm solo."

"Me too. We're soloists!" Sam high-fived me again.

Suddenly, a towering woman came up from behind and wrapped her arm around Sam's shoulder.

"We must go, *now!* Special, emergency team meeting. We need our point guard!"

As Sam disappeared into the sea of raucous celebration, she held up her hand and waved, and I did the same back.

*

I was back to working doubles at Luncheonette. It was as if I'd never left Castleton. But of course, I had left, and I had returned—with Wally, whom I'd gotten some dishwashing shifts. My parents were on their honeymoon, so there was plenty of room. Wally loved Luncheonette, especially the pre- and post-shift meals, and he fit in immediately. In fewer than two days, the entire kitchen staff was calling one another duuude in three or four languages.

Exactly ten days before Christmas, precisely at noon, four relatively downscale cars, at least by Castleton's ridiculous standards, pulled up just outside Luncheonette. A small herd of serious-looking men and women wearing black suits, sporting short haircuts stepped out of their cars and walked aggressively through Luncheonette's doors. The six men and two women flashed their badges to Mr. Nillson. I was stationed across the room, so I couldn't hear what was said. But I surmised that these men and women were with the Buildings Department, and they were checking for overcapacity. It happened every few years. Other than that they were a nuisance, I knew nothing about building inspections. However, eight inspectors seemed excessive. It also seemed quite odd that the building inspectors had hand-guns attached to their waists. As the inspectors proceeded to walk through Luncheonette, I expected the inspectors to start counting patrons—or do whatever building inspectors do—but they didn't. Instead, they walked directly to Mr. and Mrs. Z's table of six and stopped. The Zs were with their two sons and daughter, who were all in college, yes, *it* schools, and their six-year-old son, Lil' Z, who was being *it* school groomed. The inspectors addressed Mr. Z.

What did Mr. Z have to do with overcapacity?

Mr. Z stood up slowly, looked longingly at Mrs. Z and his kids, and turned around, placing his arms behind his back as the inspectors handcuffed him. I read Mr. Z's lips:

"I'm sorry." The Zs stayed seated and remained silent. As the inspectors escorted Mr. Z out, his head bowed, Luncheonette fell deathly silent.

Somehow, Lil' Z evaded the agents and ran in front of his father and embraced him, firmly planting his cheek just below his father's chest. Mr. Z was cuffed, so he was unable to embrace his son. After a long moment, two of the agents gently pried Lil' Z away from his father and escorted him back to his family. Before he was taken away, Mr. Z scanned Luncheonette. He had an unforgettable, pained expression. I knew this face. It was a version of the face I'd worn at Luncheonette. It was shame.

Moments after Mr. Z was whisked away, the hush at Luncheonette gradually lifted. There was fine food to be consumed. And whatever was going on with Mr. Z would work itself out, because everything always worked itself out in Castleton.

I assumed that the Zs would evacuate the premises immediately after Mr. Z's abrupt removal, but they quietly finished their meals without a word, and then they calmly walked out the door as if it were just another day.

As I filled water glasses and cleared tables, I couldn't rid myself of Mr. Z's pained, humiliated expression. During break, I retreated to a men's room stall and stared at the bathroom floor.

Back out on the restaurant floor, I attempted to piece together what had transpired. If Mr. Nillson knew anything, he wasn't saying. I assumed Mr. Z was in some sort of trouble for his financial work. Someone in Castleton was arrested for insider trading or something of that nature every few years. I never thought much of it. Castleton was my world, but it wasn't. My parents were middle school teachers. We were the Castleton help.

When I got home from Luncheonette, I slept soundly, but I was awoken by a text.

Dorian.

Read The Chronicle NOW!

And there it was: *The Castleton Chronicle*'s headline blared "MEET THE CHEATLETONS!" There was a full-page photo of Mr. Z being taken away in cuffs. Mr. Z's arrest had absolutely nothing to do with his financial work. The men and women in black suits were FBI agents. *The Chronicle* reported that Mr. Z was one of a dozen arrested as part of a long-running sting operation. Mr. Z and the others were alleged to have made bribes to improve their children's college entrance test scores. I read the names of those arrested. I read it five times to confirm.

Mr. and Mrs. Silversmith had been arrested.

Their mug shots were posted along with the other alleged perpetrators. No, this couldn't be true. Rosemary didn't cheat. She didn't need to. She had the grades. Test taking wasn't Rosemary's thing, but she was fine. Besides all that, Rosemary was a legacy at her *it* school. Before the game was even played, it was rigged for her. Rosemary just had to knock down a layup. I called Dorian for an explanation, for anything, but she had nothing.

*

Just when I thought they were just about gone, just when I was making real progress, they returned full force.

The pangs.

Rosemary needed me more than ever. And I needed to be there for her. I called. But her phone was disconnected. I texted.

I'm here for you. Call me.

It didn't go through. I emailed. No reply. Rosemary's Instagram had vanished.

One day before my shift, I pulled a Berkowitz. I biked over to the Silversmith's. No cars were in the driveway, and the shades were down, the lights off. Their cars were probably in their spacious garage. I didn't want to deal with Rosemary's parents, especially now, but I forced myself to knock on their front door.

No answer.

I walked around to the backyard. Rosemary's shades were down. No wheelbarrow.

A few days later, *The Castleton Chronicle* ran a front-page article on "The Cheatleton Twelve," the nickname they had given to the parents arrested. Jake Simmons aka The Taliban Kid was at the center of it. Jake had made a deal with the feds. In exchange for leniency, TTK gave up a college consultant known as The Master Mind, real name Herbert Pinner, who allegedly boosted test scores fraudulently and bribed college admissions officers to help kids get into *it* schools.

Pinner was a former country club golf pro who became an inventor after his hips gave out. He'd gone to a wannabe *it* school on a golf scholarship. Pinner's best-known creation, a cure for hangovers, failed miserably after the scientific establishment ruled that he was essentially selling dyed tap water with sugar and lemon in a fancy bottle. When he was not creating bad products, Pinner paid the bills by working as an SAT tutor. Eventually, he turned to college consulting, which was more lucrative than tutoring and less time consuming. Apparently, Pinner was quite good at what he did. For him to even talk to you, he required a $20,000 retainer. Unfortunately, it wasn't nearly enough to pay for

Pinner's gambling addiction. Jake got connected to Pinner through his uncle, a bookie. When Pinner couldn't cover his debt to Jake's uncle, he offered Jake his college consulting services.

Pinner invented TTK.

He came up with the Taliban affiliation, and he arranged for Jake to come to Castleton. Davis Palmer was one of Pinner's clients too.

And so was Rosemary.

Before I even finished reading, I called Dorian.

"What do you think?" she asked before I could get a word in.

"I need to find Rosemary."

"Why?"

"We're friends."

"She didn't treat you like one."

True, but now was not the time to address that.

"I know, but I need to find her. Have you heard anything?"

"I have no idea where she is, but I've heard some things," Dorian said ominously.

"What did you hear?" I reluctantly asked.

"You really want to know?"

"I'm asking."

"I heard that guy, whatever-his-name-is, broke up with her. He didn't even do that. He completely ghosted her."

"It was nothing."

"Nothing that lasted four months."

I was no longer listening. I wasn't breathing.

"Four months?" I somehow managed.

"Well, my friend said that they were inseparable by the third day of school."

"Third day of school?" I shouted.

"You're a smart guy Dylan. Are you really that surprised?"

"Yes . . . no. Yes. I don't know."

"I'm sorry."

I was devastated. I was embarrassed. No, I wasn't smart. I'd been played—or I'd played myself. Or both.

"I'm not so smart."

"Yes, you are."

"If I was, you wouldn't have to tell me."

"You see. That's a very smart thing to say."

I took deep, long breath.

"Well, we were seeing other people," I finally managed.

"Please don't be mad."

"I won't." I was.

At Rosemary. At myself. It was one big lie. Was there ever even an us?

Rosemary was with Neil the entire time. As much as it stung, I could finally say his name.

Yeah, I was stronger now.

Still, the facts were the facts, and they were devastating. When I got her photo with that note from my parents, she was with Neil. When her parents crashed into that twig or branch or whatever it was, she was with Neil. When she sang my Mars song to me, she was with Neil. I was stuck in the corner, and the barrage of punches wouldn't stop. Yeah, I was stronger, but I was still Dylan Mills and part of me still belonged to Rosemary. And she'd broken me, again, and it hurt. Bad. I just didn't know if I'd be right again. Ever.

*

I was at another party I didn't want to be at. Yeah, I was back where I swore I'd never go again: the Castle. But I wanted answers and someone at the Castle might know something.

No one knew anything, or if they did, they weren't talking.

Rosemary had ghosted the world—and this world didn't seem to care, at least on this unseasonably warm evening. Everyone at the Castle cared about downing beers and the streaking video. It was as if I was their long-lost, fun high school friend. I lasted almost an hour before taking off. I used my usual out: I had to work early the next day at Luncheonette. It wasn't a lie.

But I didn't want to go home. Wally was working late, and he wouldn't be home for a while. I went to Nobody You Know and drank ginger ales and listened to Sinatra on their juke box until it got old. No, there was no Barry at NYK.

After I got a mozzarella and eggplant, yeah on a baguette, I walked over to the gazebo, where Rosemary and I had spent so many moments. It would be cold again tomorrow, so might as well take advantage. Yeah, it was weird to be here again alone. I was into my third bite when I was interrupted.

"What are you doing out here?" asked the angry voice in the darkness, maybe twenty-five yards away. I feared that it was an overzealous security guard. Castleton's main lawn closed at 9:00, but the curfew was rarely if ever enforced.

"I'm leaving," I blurted, as I started to put away my baguette.

"Don't leave on my account," said the man, who was now walking toward me.

It wasn't security. Kody was wearing the black hoodie that I'd seen him in in September, and he was carrying a brown paper bag.

"It's Dylan. Dylan Mills," I replied nervously. "What's up?"

"What's up!?" Kody repeated in a mocking tone. "You don't think I know who you are?"

Kody was unshaven and had dark circles under his eyes. He was plastered and angry. I wanted no part of this.

"How are things going?" I asked, pretending to play it cool.

Kody's alcohol breath was suffocating.

"Have you seen Rosemary around?" I asked.

It just slipped out accidentally. It was the question I was asking everyone, and I was nervous and scared.

"Are you kidding me Mills?"

"No, I haven't—"

"Why are you asking me?" Kody interrupted before aggressively taking a step toward me. For a moment, I thought he might take a swing at me—but he just stared at me. "She's *your* girlfriend."

Kody was in the dark. He had no clue that there was no longer an us.

"She's not my—"

Kody wasn't listening.

"Rosemary Silversmith?" Kody exhaled, as if he'd just unburdened himself of a heavy weight. "I think about her all the time, but I haven't said her name in the longest time, at least to an actual person." Kody released a sad laugh. "No, I haven't seen that Cheatleton around. She ruined my life. . . . You, Dylan Mills, ruined my life!"

"How did I ruin your life?"

"Don't play innocent here."

"I'm not—"

"You stole my girlfriend."

"I didn't. We were friends and . . ."

I stopped myself because I wasn't sure what else to say and whatever I said probably wouldn't make a difference.

"And what Dylan Mills?" Kody yelled. "And what Dylan Mills?" he yelled louder, saliva spraying into the air. "And what Dylan Mills?"

He hated me.

"I'm sorry," I offered meekly. There was nothing to apologize for, or maybe there was.

"Well, she dumped me for you. You're the winner."

Did I hear correctly? The winner was telling me that I was a winner. Kody sat down on the opposite end of the bench, took a long swig out of whatever was in his brown paper bag, and closed his eyes and didn't say a word.

"Do you want half of this?" I finally offered.

When in doubt, offer food, good food. After too many Luncheonette shifts, I have that sliver of advice to offer.

Also, if Kody was eating, he wouldn't punch me.

"No, no thanks."

"You sure? Eggplant mozzarella. It's pretty awesome."

He looked it over.

"You sure you don't mind?"

"It's all you," I said handing him a half.

"Thanks." The eggplant mozzarella seemed to calm Kody and sober him.

"We haven't been together for a while," I finally said breaking the silence. "She dumped me too."

As he took this in, Kody gave me a long look.

"I didn't know," he said empathetically. "Sorry 'bout that."

"I thought everyone knew."

"Well, I didn't," Kody snapped, embarrassed, as if I was asking him details of a party he hadn't been invited to.

Kody stood up and started to walk away.

"See you around Dylan Mills. I got to get a life."

Kody disappeared into the darkness, leaving me alone on the bench with his brown paper bag.

*

Three days before Christmas, during another double at Luncheonette, "Unknown Number" flashed up on my phone.

My heart started racing.

It was probably another car warranty call—or maybe, Rosemary was surfacing, finally. When I finally could steal a moment, I listened to the voice mail in the restroom.

"Mr. Dylan Mills," said the unfamiliar voice.

Yeah, it was another car warranty hustle.

"It's Marcia Davenport."

She was back! Marcia Davenport was the admissions officer from the wannabe *it* school, which had wait-listed me for its wait-list before telling me to get lost.

Now, suddenly, I was found.

Yeah, I'd called Ms. Davenport a few times—OK more than a few—to reiterate my interest in her school. She'd always told me I was on the fence until she ultimately informed me I was on the wrong side of the fence.

What could this woman want now? She couldn't tell me to get lost again. Or maybe this was all one big mistake. Either way, I braced myself.

"We're happy to say that we have a place in the freshman class opening for the spring semester. Congratulations! Your persistence paid off. If you're still interested, please call me as soon as possible."

I listened to the voice mail at least a half dozen times. Yes! I was in. I was finally in! Kody was correct: I was a winner. I washed my face and hands and walked outside confidently, a changed man. I was a changed man. Of course, Ms. Davenport had accepted me. But it was more than that. I'd made honors at North South. And I finally got my driver's license. Wally was a phenomenal driving instructor.

But no one at Luncheonette treated me differently. As I bussed, I thought to myself, "These diners have no idea that an *it* school busboy is taking their plates and filling their water glasses."

After the double, I walked back home with Wally and told him about the Ms. Davenport call.

"You're not going to take it, right?" he asked before I could finish.

"Well, I was planning on it," I said carefully.

"You think it's better than North South?"

"I wouldn't say it's better, just different. It was one of my first choices."

"It was above North South?"

"Yeah," I admitted, still treading lightly. "It was."

"But if it's not better, why would you go?" Wally almost whined, something I don't recall him doing before.

Walter Johnson was not a whiner.

"I don't know," I said, backpedaling, my eyes staring down. "I just want to give it a shot."

When I finally made eye contact with Wally, his eyes were watery. For the entire semester, I did everything in my power to not cry in front of motorcycle dude Wally. Now he was the one tearing up.

"What's wrong?"

"I'm going to miss you, duuude."

"We're going to stay in touch."

Right after I said it, I regretted it. His foster families had always promised this but rarely delivered. When I dreamt of something like this happening, I always envisioned it as one of the happiest days of my life. Instead, I felt plain rotten.

But I was getting what I'd asked for multiple times, and I was accepting the offer. Early the next morning, I left a voice mail for Ms. Davenport and formally accepted. I also explained that I needed a few days because my parents were out of the country, and I needed to discuss financial details with them. I already knew that Ms. Davenport's school would be quite an expense. I'd have to go through my entire savings, and it would be a massive burden to get the remainder. My mother would probably have to ask for a gift from her wealthy aunt. After I broke the news to Wally, I was already having second thoughts. Now, as I pondered the financials, I was wondering if Ms. Davenport's *it* school was the right call.

Besides Wally, I didn't tell anyone. I thought the acceptance would change everything. It did, and it didn't. I was still working at Luncheonette. Wally was still my best friend, at least, I think he was. He never said it, but he was upset with me. I couldn't blame him. I was upset with me. When the excitement of the acceptance settled, I faced the reality: The only reason I wanted to go to Ms. Davenport's school was to increase my status in Castleton. Yeah, I'd come a long way, but I'd also gone nowhere.

And yeah, I was still trying to track down Rosemary.

According to Dorian, the rumor was that Rosemary's parents went away on an already planned vacation to visit their wealthy, politically connected relatives. We assumed that Rosemary went along. With their criminal charges pending, it seemed like the vacation from hell.

*

After my Christmas Eve brunch shift, I had a rare moment of downtime, which I didn't want. I needed Ms. Davenport school money, and I didn't need any spare time to obsess over Rosemary and her parents. Anyway, Luncheonette had shut down early and was closed on Christmas. A day earlier, Wally had left Castleton to celebrate with cousins, and my parents, well, they were still honeymooning. Yeah, I'll never get used to saying that. Anyway, I took off in my father's economy car and started driving without a destination. I needed the practice. I found myself eight miles away from Calm Lake, where Rosemary's family had their cottage.

Yeah, Rosemary had pulled me in yet again.

When I drove into the Silversmith driveway, it was already dusk, and Calm Lake was foggy, almost recognizable.

It seemed like years since Rosemary and I were here together gazing at the moon-lit sky. No one was around, but I knocked on the door anyway.

No answer.

I placed my ear to the door. Silence.

"Hello! Is anyone home?"

Nothing.

I turned the knob. The door was open. Not a total surprise. Everyone in Castleton kept their doors open because nothing bad happened in Castleton. But this wasn't Castleton.

"Hello! Hello!" I repeated as I stood at the doorway scanning the living room, which was cluttered with take-out cartons, empty liquor and soda bottles, and clothing.

Rosemary's clothing.

And I couldn't ignore the heavy marijuana fumes. She'd been here. Recently. Rosemary wasn't away on vacation. My heart was already at full speed. I proceeded cautiously. There wasn't much to inspect. It was a single-floor, three-bedroom cottage, and the rooms were small. It was very modest, at least by insane Castleton standards. As I cautiously inspected the mess, I was terrified that I might walk into something too horrible to fathom. The beds were bare, no sheets. Marijuana joint remnants sat in a few ashtrays.

I exhaled.

This wasn't a crime scene. Rosemary wasn't here now.

When I relieved myself, I noticed that the bathroom window was wide open. Immediately, I ran outside, which was now pitch black. I turned on my headlights. Nothing. I walked up to the water's edge; same result. From the main road, I faintly heard an engine struggling to start. I cautiously ran through the driveway toward the noise.

Rosemary's car was at a standstill. She'd parked in the woods, where the Silversmiths had cleared out an area so guests could park when they had gatherings, which I wasn't invited to. I looked in the driver's window, and there she was, almost unrecognizable. Rosemary had a terrified expression on her face, and she was in her underwear.

"What do you want from me?" she screamed. "Why can't you leave me alone?"

"I just wanted to make sure that you're all right."

Rosemary started to bawl hysterically. Any anger was immediately replaced with a need to help.

"It's going to be okay," I assured. "Everything's going to be fine."

Of course, I had no clue if that was truly the case.

After Rosemary calmed down, she put on my heavy-duty North South sweatshirt, which I'd been wearing, and I carried her to the cottage. It wasn't difficult. She was considerably lighter, and I was substantially stronger thanks to Wally's workouts. I walked as fast as I possibly could, and I didn't stop until I placed her down on the couch and covered her with a blanket. I got a good look at her in the light. Rosemary was no longer her shiny self. She was thin and shockingly pale, her hair was scraggly, and her teeth were no longer pristine white. And her scent was no longer her scent.

"I didn't know who you were out there," Rosemary cried. "I was scared."

"I understand," I said softly.

"How'd you get here?"

"I drove."

"You drove?"

"Yeah, I drove."

"You got your license?"

"Yes. I'm not very good, but I'm working on it."

After Rosemary showered, she laid back down on the couch in my North South sweatshirt. I prepared tea and cleaned up the clutter. She'd done the same for me so many times before.

"You're always here for me," Rosemary whispered between sips.

"We're here for each other," I replied instinctively.

It wasn't true, but I wanted it to be.

"I want to tell you something," Rosemary whispered slowly.

"Okay," I replied slowly, uncertain if I wanted to hear it.

"Everyone thinks I cheated, but I didn't. I'm not a cheater."

"Everyone doesn't think you cheated."

Yeah, I was in no position to speak for everyone.

"Yes, they do."

"I don't."

"You! You don't count," Rosemary whispered. "You'll love me through anything."

Yeah, I let that marinate.

Rosemary eventually drifted off.

I couldn't. I looked around the Silversmith's cottage. When I was at North South in my closet, under my lavender sheets, buried in textbooks, hiding from the world and waiting for her, I used to dream about being here. Just us.

But I didn't want to be here now.

I wanted to sleep in my own bed and prepare for my next phase at my *it* school. But Rosemary needed me, period. And even if I wanted to, I couldn't leave. A mediocre new driver shouldn't be on unfamiliar roads at night. I lay down on one of the bedroom mattresses under a blanket, but Rosemary's words kept reverberating.

You'll love me through anything.

I wanted Rosemary to be wrong. But she wasn't. I'd love her, even when I shouldn't and even when I didn't want to.

*

"Merry Christmas!" Rosemary whispered as she stared directly into my eyes and petted my hair, something I don't recall her ever doing.

"What time is it?" I managed between a yawn.

"It's almost 6:00," Rosemary replied before kissing my forehead, which was nice but weird.

"I'm going to take you home."

"Reporters are stalking my house."

"No one's there."

"How do you know?"

"I've been there every day, sometimes twice a day."

"You were concerned about me?"

"Of course I was concerned about you!" I said, raising my voice, sounding a lot like my father. " I . . ." And then I stopped myself.

"What? What?"

"Nothing. I just . . ."

"You don't love me any—?"

"We need to get you home," I interrupted. "You can't stay here. It's not good for you."

"You don't have to love me anymore," Rosemary replied softly. "I understand."

She didn't.

After more tidying up, we returned to Castleton. I drove. I wasn't comfortable with Rosemary behind the wheel. Rosemary was impressed with my slow, methodical driving on the empty road, or at least she said she was. I wasn't.

"It's a witch hunt!" Rosemary finally uttered.

"Okay," I said in a measured voice. "Well, what's going to happen now?"

"Our lawyers say that the government has no case. They can prove only that we paid for a college consultant, and who doesn't hire a consultant in Castleton?"

I didn't, but I kept that to myself.

"They're hoping to scare us into pleading guilty."

"How much did you pay this consultant?" I asked, attempting to not sound like I was in interrogation mode.

"About $40,000 altogether, I think." It was about half of what one of my parents made a year. "Actually, it might've been $50,000. But it was over the course of two years."

"Will there be a trial?"

"No one can say for sure, but the lawyers are expecting the charges to be dropped after New Year's. We just have to wait."

"And then everything'll be fine."

"No, nothing's fine! They've ruined my life! Look, I've made up my mind. I'm not going back!"

"What are you saying?"

"I'm not going back to school."

"You must. It's your school. It's your parents' school."

"I can't."

"Were you expelled?"

"No, well, not yet."

"Suspended?"

"Not yet. Everyone's on break."

"I was suspended."

"You?" Rosemary managed to somehow laugh. "For what?"

"You saw the video."

"They should give you a trophy or something for that. It was hilarious."

"Yeah, a trophy for streaking and falling on my face," I deadpanned. "You should go back to school."

"I can't. I'm innocent, but everyone will look at me like I'm a Cheatleton," Rosemary sighed.

"You're no Cheatleton."

I couldn't say Cheatleton without smiling. Rosemary managed a small one too.

"I have no friends."

"We're on break, and you got rid of your phone."

"I learned that from you."

"I'm just full of bright ideas. . . . You'll get new friends, and the old ones will come back, eventually. And who cares what everyone thinks?"

"You don't care what everyone thinks?"

"I'm getting better."

"You know something?"

"No," I said. "I really don't. I don't know anything!"

Rosemary playfully tapped my shoulder.

"Tell me. How'd you get so funny?"

"Genetics; upbringing in a contentious, overbearing household. I take zero credit."

"I love you," Rosemary blurted out.

It was a jarring pronouncement. I stared into Rosemary's large green eyes staring at me.

"I love you too."

It wasn't a lie, but it was different, like I was saying it to a different person.

Who was this Rosemary?

But Rosemary needed to hear it now—more than ever.

"Will they take me at North South?" Rosemary finally asked in a low, sincere voice.

"What? You're joking," I laughed.

"I'm serious. It worked for you. Berkowitz! He sounds super cool."

"Berkowitz, yeah, he's awesome, but he'll be the first to tell you that he's not cool."

"He's so not cool. He's cool."

"That's one way of looking at it."

Rosemary turned toward me and looked at me with a serious, somber expression.

"I know it will take time, lots of time, but I want to make things right between *us*."

For so long, I wanted to hear this. Now, I didn't know how to reply.

I wanted to say, "But I'm not going back to North South."

I wanted to say, "But there is no *us*."

I wanted to say, "But I love you and you lied to me!"

But I said none of it. None of it felt right, at least now. I'd get around to it, eventually, maybe.

Or probably.

Or definitely.

I wasn't just talking about stuff now. I was doing it.

I couldn't leave Rosemary alone—and I didn't want to be alone. It was Christmas. I found a supermarket open in an adjacent town. I made a roast and sweet potato mash, which I picked up from spying on the Luncheonette chefs. Despite my uncertainty about, well, everything, I spent Christmas at Rosemary's in Castleton. We laid out on the carpet in the Silversmith's living room and ate too much and watched dumb movies we didn't really want to watch again until we dozed off.

In the middle of the night, Rosemary asked me to get an extra blanket from her bedroom closet. When I grabbed it from the shelf, a folder fell to the floor and papers slipped out. "Operation 13th Grade" was printed on the folder's cover in Rosemary's unmistakable handwriting. I smiled at the title. I used to joke that I was graduating to thirteenth grade. There were all sorts of documents I never wanted to see again, ever: transcripts, applications, requirements, and recommendations. But there was something I hadn't seen, a college application essay titled "Swimming Underwater."

> Underwater is a special, peaceful universe—away from social media and phones. It's a safe place, and it allows me to concentrate and focus on the person I aspire to be, not the person everyone expects. It works—way better than yoga.

I couldn't read any more. I was confused. And I was appalled and hurt that Rosemary hadn't told me that she was writing about underwater swimming. Underwater swimming was my thing—or at least it used to be.

When we were us, we shared everything. At least I thought we did. Why was she hiding this?

If Rosemary could lie about that, she could lie about anything.

Rosemary *was* a Cheatleton!

JANUARY

Rosemary was innocent!

Or at least her parents weren't found guilty. Shortly after New Year's, the charges against Rosemary's parents were dropped, just as her lawyers predicted. For one, Rosemary's SAT proctor had vanished, which wasn't all that unusual. It's a temporary position. Employers hire temps to work—and then go away. Rosemary hadn't taken her test in Castleton. She took it close to Calm Lake where there were no Castleton distractions. Sure, that might sound suspicious, but it made perfect sense. I would've done the same. I should've done the same.

According to *The Castleton Chronicle*, a few of the other alleged Cheatletons also had their charges dropped. Others though weren't as fortunate. They plead guilty in hopes of receiving leniency. Mr. Z was hoping for six months, out in two, at least that was the rumor. It was alleged that he'd paid almost a million dollars to have his children's college entrance exams rigged. Unlike the Silversmiths, Mr. Z made the mistake of discussing it over the phone.

As Mr. Z awaited sentencing, not surprisingly, he didn't show his face at Luncheonette. While I stopped hearing his voice in my head, I thought of him. I recalled all the times I hated Mr. Z. It seemed silly now. Mr. Z was just another pretender, another fraud. I wasn't judging. There had already been too much of that.

I finally did what I'd been putting off: calling Berkowitz and letting him know that I was transferring. It was break, and there were no office hours, so I expected voice mail. When he answered, I should not have been surprised. Berkowitz's office hours were 24/7, 365. He was excited to hear from me and before I could get a word in, he asked about Luncheonette and my family. He wanted to know how Mick Jagger—his nickname for Wally—had worked out at Luncheonette. As far as transferring, I'd get to that. I just couldn't bring myself to tell him.

I checked in with Rosemary every day. When I called, she always picked up immediately. It was a mental health check-up call. When I stopped by, I went through the front door. I strongly suspected that the Silversmiths weren't receiving many visitors. Her parents were nicer than ever—and I didn't have to bring over any white chocolates or mow their lawn. They invited me to sit on the couch and asked whether I wanted to stay for dinner. While she was apprehensive, Rosemary was returning to her *it* school.

A day before Rosemary was to leave, we agreed to meet at Castleton's gazebo. When I arrived, she was waiting.

For a moment, Rosemary and I stood and stared at one another without a word. Rosemary had returned to her Instagram shine and then some. She'd gained some weight back and looked healthy. She'd have no problem attracting followers. I know. I'd been one. Sure, Rosemary looked almost perfect to the outside world, but I knew better. When I looked into her green eyes now, I saw a beautiful woman, but I also saw anxiety.

"So this is it?" Rosemary finally said as she bit down on her lip.

"Another semester, another goodbye," I answered.

I didn't know what to say, but I shouldn't have said something so hokey. But there was too much to say, and where would I begin? Rosemary had made me and my parents feel special. Nothing else mattered. It didn't matter where I went to school. It didn't matter when I grew up—or if I ever grew up. Or what I became. When Rosemary went away, it shattered us.

But it also gave us a chance to start over.

How's that going?

I don't know. It's too early to say. Anyway, there was too much to say, so we continued to just stare at one another. It was all or nothing, and I chose nothing.

For now.

"Why didn't you tell me you saw 'Operation 13th Grade'?" Rosemary finally asked. I was caught off guard, momentarily speechless.

"How did you know I saw it?"

"I didn't but when I returned the blanket, it was out of place. I figured you had."

"I don't know. There was a lot going on. I just wanted you to feel better."

"I was going to tell you. I just didn't know how. And then I just never got around to it. I was embarrassed. I was embarrassed about a lot of things," Rosemary explained, her voice trailing off. "Are you mad?"

"I was at first, but I'm also flattered."

"Really?"

"I guess I inspired you. But I wish you would've told me. I used to feel like we told each other everything."

"I'm sorry. I'm so sorry," Rosemary said as a tear rolled down her face. "I messed up. I messed up a lot of things."

"Don't be sorry," I said almost instinctively. "Make it better!"

"I will make it better," Rosemary declared sincerely. "I promise."

I believed her.

"And I will too."

"You're already doing it. North South honor roll. Amazing."

"Thanks."

"I have a new roommate!"

I felt awkward again. I hadn't met Rosemary's old roommate.

"Is she cool?"

"Can't say for sure, but I'm not getting a creep vibe."

I got a text, and I checked my phone.

Mr. Nillson.

Someone called out, and he needed me ASAP.

"It's work. They need me to come in now."

"Can you just stay a few more minutes?" Rosemary asked in a needy voice.

"It's an emergency. I can't."

We embraced, holding on to one another tighter than perhaps we ever had. It felt like a goodbye—a real goodbye. As I ran out of the gazebo and onto the empty sidewalk, I felt Rosemary's eyes following me. I didn't look back.

*

A week later, my parents woke up early to send me off. We group hugged before I jumped into my economy car, which I'd purchased with some of my *it* school money.

No, I didn't do it. I couldn't.

A few days earlier, I'd notified Ms. Davenport that I wouldn't be accepting her offer. Yeah, it felt nice to be the one rejecting, rather than the other way around. But it wasn't about that. North South wasn't perfect. I wasn't. Nothing is—not even Castleton as much as it tries; that's for sure. As I obsessed over my decision, I kept thinking of Berkowitz . . . Wally. . . . And I kept repeating Mr. Wells's words to me on the ride back from the hospital.

"We're building something special here."

We were.

I drove like a tortoise, and it took a good seven-plus hours to get to North South, which had just gotten hammered with a massive snow dump. I arrived at the North Pole's parking lot an hour or so before sundown. It was desolate.

Maybe everyone else had transferred.

I did hear that the Dandruff Duo eloped and moved to the Caribbean. I dropped off my stuff, put on some heavy clothing, and went for a walk to investigate. I saw no one, but I heard voices coming from the lake.

An enormous crowd was out in force. Kids were sliding down the hill onto the ice. A brave few were catching air off an enormous jump. A half dozen or so vert discers were skating and flinging a frisbee. Quarters was supervising the construction of a massive, nonbinary snow creature. Sherbert and Jake Simmons, yes, formerly The Taliban Kid, were intently listening. After his scandal, Jake was expelled from his *it* school. *It* school or not, Jake was going places. Jake didn't need college. College needed Jake. I told Mr. Wells about him, and Mr. Wells wound up actively recruiting him to come to North South.

As I walked up the hill, I spotted Sam in the distance hanging out with her teammates. When we made eye contact, we smiled warmly at one another. I would've gone over, but she seemed busy. When Wally saw me at the top of the hill, he did a double take. We quickly embraced before his smile turned apprehensive.

"I guess you're here to pick up your stuff."

"I'm not picking up my stuff."

"You're not picking up your stuff?"

"I'm not going anywhere."

"What happened?"

"Home is home, and this is home." Wally's face brightened, which made mine do the same.

"You wanna take a ride?"

"Yeah. And I want to try that jump."

"Go for it!"

At the hill's highest point, I walked back about fifteen yards, so I could get a running start.

"That jump is pretty intense, duuude," Wally cautioned. "Take it easy."

"I will."

I didn't.

I ran as fast as I could. When I got to the hill's decline, I dove headfirst. I was moving—faster than I drove, at least it felt that way. It was a rush. When I hit the jump, I got more air than I expected or wanted. I wish someone took a photo. I came down hard and slid onto the icy lake and kept going. When I finally stopped, I was almost at the other side of the lake. What a ride! For a few moments, I just lay on my stomach admiring the North South campus. It looked like the gymnasium was just about complete.

"Are you okay?"

When I saw that it was Sam, I immediately stood up.

"I'm good."

"You really went for it. Are you going to take another run?"

"I think I'm going to keep it on the ground."

"Well, what's next?"

I didn't know. For a moment, I just admired Sam's smile.

"Do you want to get a hot chocolate and maybe something to eat?"

"At the cafeteria?"

"No, somewhere uptown. I have my car."

"You got a car?"

"Yeah."

"Would this be like a date?"

"It would definitely be a date."

"Well then, I'm in."

ACKNOWLEDGEMENTS

Writing is a solitary endeavor, but I had a solid team of unique individuals encouraging me – even when I didn't hear or see them. Forgive any name misspellings. It might have been a while. Thank you Rachel Bloom, Stephen Breimer, Bruce Cohn Curtis, Grace Dougherty, Brett Eidman, Kevin Hennebry, James Hill, Julie Hill, Mark David Hill, Hunter Hoberman, Jason Hollins, Doug Katz, Tom Kearns, David Krauss, Mike Kylis, Meg Minard, Craig Newmark, Hank Owenmark, Lauren Owenmark, Adam Paul, Scott Pollack, Patrick Seacor, Howard Smith, Brad Trackman, Dave Waltner and Whit Washing.

Pat Bartnicki: Thank you for everything. With your support, I could've made it to Brother Rice. Jennifer Bruno is quite simply my Audrey Hepburn. Fontana, no last required, you're a star. [Peter] Fontana has gone above and beyond and beyond. Leorah Gavidor is a killer copy editor. Nicole Hirschman's expert copy editing and shrewd feedback made this better. Kenny Hoberman was the best three-month BFF I've ever had, period. Caroline Knecht looked at an early draft and treated it as if it were her own. I don't know where I'd be without Lampert's incessant optimism and relentless positivity. Jonny Lampert is firmly on this bandwagon, in the driver's seat. Back in the day, Randall Lane sent me off into the pro wrestling trenches and other brutal, fun places. Rob Lombardi is an awesome manager, no leather jacket required. God created man. William Margold created himself. Amen. Louie Max inspired this epic, among other things. Mike Sager delivered this to the finish line and out into the world. My parents did the same for me. I'm eternally grateful.

ABOUT THE AUTHOR

Jon Hart is the author of *Man versus Ball: One Ordinary Guy and His Extraordinary Sports Adventures* (Potomac Books). *Party School* is his first novel.

ABOUT THE PUBLISHER

The Sager Group was founded in 1984. In 2012 it was chartered as a multimedia content brand, with the intent of empowering those who create art—an umbrella beneath which makers can pursue, and profit from, their craft directly, without gatekeepers. TSG publishes books; ministers to artists and provides modest grants; and produces documentary, feature, and commercial films. By harnessing the means of production, The Sager Group helps artists help themselves. For more information, please see www. TheSagerGroup.net.

MORE BOOKS FROM
THE SAGER GROUP

The Swamp: Deceit and Corruption in the CIA
An Elizabeth Petrov Thriller (Book 1)
by Jeff Grant

Chains of Nobility: Brotherhood of the Mamluks (Book 1-3)
by Brad Graft

Meeting Mozart: A Novel Drawn from the Secret
Diaries of Lorenzo Da Ponte
by Howard Jay Smith

Death Came Swiftly: Novel About the Tay Bridge Disaster of 1879
by Bill Abrams

A Boy and His Dog in Hell: And Other Stories
by Mike Sager

Miss Havilland: A Novel
by Gay Daly

The Orphan's Daughter: A Novel
by Jan Cherubin

Lifeboat No. 8: Surviving the Titanic
by Elizabeth Kaye

Hunting Marlon Brando: A True Story
by Mike Sager

See our entire library at TheSagerGroup.net

THE SAGER GROUP

Artifex Te Adiuva

Made in United States
Troutdale, OR
12/02/2024

25701819R00141